DEAD AND BURIED

LEIGHANN DOBBS

This is a work of fiction.

None of it is real. All names, places, and events are products of the author's imagination. Any resemblance to real names, places, or events are purely coincidental, and should not be construed as being real.

1
———

Morgan Blackmoore slipped out the kitchen door of the seaside mansion she shared with her sisters in the sleepy town of Noquitt, Maine. Stretching her arms over her head she closed her eyes, and took a deep breath, relishing the sting of the salty sea air and the warmth of the early morning sun on her face.

She turned east toward the Atlantic Ocean where the sun was just coming up. Her cat, Belladonna, rustled in the leaves at her feet and a group of seagulls made a cacophony of sound to her right. There seemed to be more gulls than usual this morning. Morgan opened her eyes, turning toward the sound.

Her heart skipped a beat when she saw the flock of gulls circling. There were *way* too many birds.

Something must have attracted them and Morgan had a feeling it wasn't anything good.

She picked her way through her herb garden toward the edge of the cliff, Belladonna trotting along at her side, while the seagulls circled and flapped noisily above. Her stomach felt like she'd swallowed a lead ball, and her mind conjured up a scene from the old Hitchcock classic, *The Birds*, as she approached the point of land where the channel leading to the cove on the right of her house met with the ocean on the left.

Belladonna sprinted ahead of her and poked her head over the side of the cliff, then looked up at Morgan with her ice-blue eyes.

"Mew."

"What is it?" Morgan craned her neck over the side, but whatever was attracting the seagulls was hidden behind an outcropping of rock about seven feet down.

She sighed, rubbed her palms on her faded jeans and put one foot tentatively on the slope of the cliff. Unlike the ocean side of the cliff, which was a straight drop, the point was more gradual with outcroppings of rock that she could navigate on the way down.

She balanced herself by grabbing onto a rock while her foot grappled for placement. Her heart jerked wildly as she dislodged some small stones, creating a mini rockslide. Holding her breath, she watched the rocks plunge almost one hundred feet into the turbulent ocean below. If she fell, it would mean a painful and certain death.

"Meow!"

Morgan looked up at the white cat who was staring down at her. "Yeah, easy for you to say. How come you're not down here with your perfect balance and nine lives?"

Belladonna just blinked at her lazily from above, then trotted off.

"Okay, fine. I get it. I'm on my own." Morgan grabbed onto a tree that was growing sideways on the slope and inched over to the outcropping, her free arm grabbing onto the rock and pulling herself along until she was far enough to peer over.

She sucked in a breath, a jolt of electricity piercing her heart when her eyes found the object of the seagulls' attention.

Lying on the rocks was a man, his legs and neck bent at impossible angles. His dead eyes stared straight through her. His right arm was twisted underneath him. His left was visible and Morgan noticed an unusual black mark on the palm.

She jerked back, then whirled around and scrambled back up the slope, kicking loose stones that pinged against the rocks below in her wake. Pushing herself up onto the grass, she turned to run in the direction of her house at full speed. But instead of moving forward, she smacked straight into her biggest enemy.

Sheriff Overton.

* * *

"LEAVING THE SCENE OF THE CRIME?"

Overton glared down at her, his large belly bulging over the belt of his brown pants. Sweat trickled down his forehead under the brim of his hat.

Morgan pushed herself away from him and looked back in the direction of the cliff.

"What are you talking about? I saw the seagulls and went down to see why they were gathered there. It is, after all, my property."

Overton narrowed his eyes at her, the toothpick jutting out of the side of his mouth wiggled back and forth as his teeth ground on it. "Or you could have been down there covering something up."

Morgan's eyebrows knit together as she turned back to face him. She spread her hands. "What would

I be covering up? And how did *you* get here before I even called the police?"

"Gordy Wright saw the body on his way out to pull his lobster traps this morning. He called it in."

Morgan looked at the channel that led to Perkins Cove where most of the fishermen docked their boats. Her house sat at the very end of the channel— the point where it emptied out into the ocean so, naturally, the boats had to sail by her house to get out. Gordy always went out at sunrise and would certainly have noticed the gulls and body on the cliff.

"It's awfully suspicious in my book that a body shows up in your yard after the whole Littlefield incident," Overton said.

Morgan crossed her arms over her chest, struggling to stay calm. "You know I had nothing to do with that."

Earlier in the summer, Overton had accused Morgan of killing the town shrew, Prudence Littlefield. It had taken some clever detective work on the part of her and her sisters to find the real killer and clear Morgan's name. Even so, it seemed Overton had it in for them and Morgan could think of no good reason why.

Which was why she had to tread carefully with this dead body on the cliff. If Overton could find a way to pin it on her or one of her sisters, she was sure he would.

A noise over by the house captured her attention and she glanced over to see her sister, Fiona, hurrying toward them, her long red curls flying behind her as she walked.

"What's going on?"

"There's a body on the cliff." Morgan nodded her chin toward the point.

Fiona gasped, her eyes growing wide. "A body? Who?"

"I don't know. I saw the seagulls and went over to investigate. Never saw him before."

Overton snorted. "We'll see about that. I doubt you girls are as innocent as you want me to believe."

Fiona took a step closer to him, pulling herself up as tall as she could. "Now you see here, Overton. You can't go around accusing us of everything that happens in this town—"

"Sheriff? Where's the body."

Several members of their small town police force had come up behind them and the girls turned in their direction.

"Over here." Overton started toward the cliff then turned back toward Morgan and Fiona. "I have a sneaky suspicion there's more to this than meets the eye and I bet the two of you are right in the middle of it."

He glanced back at the officers who had continued on and were halfway to the cliff's edge. Removing the toothpick from his mouth, he jabbed it in Morgan's direction.

"You might want to call your fancy lawyer, because if I find evidence you had anything to do with this, I'm going to make sure you feel the full force of the law. This time you won't get away so easy."

Morgan watched him shove the toothpick back in his mouth and lumber off toward the cliff. She half hoped he would trip and fall right over then caught herself, realizing that would be a terrible fate, even for him.

The two girls watched him while he approached the cliff's edge when, out of nowhere, Belladonna streaked in front of him causing him to stumble and almost pitch over the side.

"Damn cat! Thing should be shot." He glared after the cat who had disappeared into the bushes.

Morgan and Fiona had to clamp their hands over their mouths to keep from laughing out loud as they walked back toward the house.

* * *

MORGAN OPENED the kitchen door and Belladonna appeared from nowhere, scooting inside ahead of them.

Fiona reached down to pet the cat. "Good girl, you want a treat?"

Belladonna walked over to her bowl and sat in front of it licking her paw, as if she were ambivalent about the treat, while Fiona got a can of tuna from the cupboard.

"I see Overton is still as big a jerk as ever," Fiona said.

"Yep. He worries me. There's no telling what he might do." Morgan peered out the back door window toward the cliff, where she could see the police department turning out in full force.

"What's going on out there?"

Morgan's sister, Celeste, stood in the doorway, her concerned gaze directed at the corner of the yard where the police were now swarming.

"There's a body on the cliff," Fiona said as she flipped open the tuna can then bent to scoop the fish into Belladonna's dish.

"Excuse me?" Celeste ruffled her short blonde hair, still wet from showering, as she walked over to the window.

"Yeah, it was weird. I saw a bunch of seagulls over by the cliff and went over to investigate and there was a guy lying on the rocks. Dead." Morgan felt a shiver go up her spine. It had been only four years since her mother had taken her own life near that same spot. This one was too close for comfort.

"Why would a dead body be in our yard?" Celeste turned her wide, ice-blue eyes on Morgan.

"That's a good question. What *would* someone be doing on the cliff?" Morgan's eyebrows creased in the middle.

"And why would someone kill him there?" Fiona asked. "Or did he die from falling off the cliff?"

Morgan pursed her lips together. "You know, I'm not exactly sure. He wasn't far down so I don't see how he could have died from a fall, but in the dark I guess he might have tripped and hit his head or some-thing. I didn't really look at him that close."

"Maybe they killed him somewhere else and dumped him there," Celeste said as she opened the double wide refrigerator and took out some spinach.

"But why?"

"I don't know," Fiona said, "I'll ask Jake later today what he knows."

"Yeah, I'm surprised he's not here." Morgan

glanced out the window looking for the handsome former detective and newest member of the Noquitt Police department. Jake Cooper had proved to be an invaluable ally when Morgan had been accused of murdering Prudence Littlefield.

Morgan smiled at the way Fiona's ice-blue eyes got all dreamy when she said Jake's name. Jake and Fiona had gotten close during the Littlefield investigation and now they were practically inseparable. Morgan tried to push down the pang of sadness she felt for herself.

Would she ever be able to find love like that again?

She'd had that kind of love once with her high school sweetheart, Luke Hunter. They'd dated into their early twenties. But Luke had decided he wanted to join the military and had broken it off with her. She hadn't seen him in over a decade and hadn't found anyone else that sparked her interest either.

Morgan remembered several weeks earlier when she'd *thought* she'd seen Luke downtown. But it hadn't been him … just someone who looked like him. Still, it had raised all those old feelings, of love and betrayal. She should be over him by now. But …

"… Morgan?" Celeste interrupted her thoughts.

"Sorry, what?"

"Did you say it was a man? What did the guy look

like?" Celeste stood in front of the juicer, a cupful of spinach and some green sprouted stuff in her hand.

Morgan's heart clenched as she thought back to the body on the cliff. "He was a big guy, blonde and muscular. Rough looking. One thing was strange though."

Celeste raised a blonde eyebrow. "What was that?"

"He had a black mark on his hand. Like a big circle. It just struck me as odd."

Celeste stood looking at Morgan, chewing her bottom lip, her brows creased with worry.

"Celeste, is something wrong?" Fiona asked.

"It's just that I had a dream about something similar." Celeste shrugged and turned back to the juicer. "Just a coincidence, I'm sure."

Morgan watched her sister, a strange feeling of foreboding starting to spread in her stomach.

"Meow."

Belladonna flopped down over by the back stairs that led to the attic, which was once servants' quarters and now housed several generations of Blackmoore family cast offs, and proceeded to clean her snow white fur.

"I guess Belladonna agrees." Morgan opened the cupboard, sifting through the herbal tea bags for chamomile. She could use something to soothe her nerves.

"Do you think we should call Delphine?" Fiona asked, referring to the lawyer who had been instrumental in shielding the girls from the threats of Overton earlier that summer.

"I think Overton was just trying to scare us. I mean, he doesn't have anything to tie us to the body, since we didn't kill him." Morgan plunked her tea cup into the microwave. "We don't even know if he actually was murdered."

"Yeah, I guess you're right." Fiona nodded. "Hey, where's Jolene?"

Celeste rolled her eyes. "Still sleeping."

Jolene, Morgan's youngest sister, had only been fourteen when their mother jumped to her death. The three older sisters had tried to raise her as best they could. She'd been a handful, but was recently starting to come around. Still, like most teens, she loved sleeping in.

"Celeste, will you let her know what's going on out there?" Fiona nodded toward the cliff. "I don't want her to wake up and panic when she sees the Noquitt Police Department in the back yard."

"Sure, I don't go into the yoga studio until noon."

Celeste ran her greens through the juicer producing a cup full of thick green goo.

"I guess we better go open the shop." Fiona turned to Morgan, car keys in her hand. "There's nothing for us to do anyway. I'll call Jake later and find out what Overton's game plan is, and if we should be worried."

Morgan shrugged. "I guess you're right."

She grabbed her tea and headed for the door, the feeling of foreboding growing stronger—whatever Overton's game plan was, Morgan was pretty sure she wasn't going to like it.

2

Morgan felt her spirits lift as Fiona pulled her truck up to their shop, *Sticks and Stones*. The old cottage that had been in the family for generations, sat at one of the highest points in their town of Noquitt, Maine. It was quaint with antique weathered cedar clapboards, crisp white trim and an abundance of flowers.

Set back in the woods, the shop was just slightly off the beaten path, but not so out of the way that it discouraged customers. In fact, the wooded location helped add to the mystique of the herbs and crystals the girls sold.

Morgan finished the last of her tea then hopped out of the truck, eager to get inside and start the day's work. She always felt content in the little cottage and she needed a little bit of contentment after the morning's events.

"We need to cut some of these roses." Fiona pointed to a thick red rose bush to the right of the porch steps which was loaded with a carpet of blooms.

"I'll do that later." Morgan bent over to smell a rose. She loved having vases full of fresh cut flowers from their garden in the shop and cutting off the blooms would keep the plant flowering all summer.

As she straightened, she felt a prickle at the back of her neck. She spun around, her stomach sinking.

Was someone watching her?

Narrowing her eyes, she scanned the woods around the shop but didn't see anything.

"What's the matter?" Fiona was standing on the porch, her hand poised in front of the electric keypad that disarmed the alarm.

"Oh nothing." Morgan shrugged. "I guess I'm just jittery from finding that body."

"No doubt."

Fiona punched in the code and went inside. Morgan followed her in, taking one last backward glance out into the woods before she turned the sign to "open" and closed the door.

Inside, the earthy smell of old wood and herbs

soothed her senses. Fiona went straight to her work-bench where an array of jewelers tools lay surrounding her latest piece—a moonstone and peridot necklace commissioned by one of their regular customers.

Morgan turned to the left where tall wooden racks with small cubby holes housed a variety of herbs. She picked out some chamomile, loaded it into a tea infuser, and heated some water on her small gas burner.

On the other side of the shop, Fiona let out a sigh. "I can't stop wondering *why* someone would turn up dead on our cliff. I mean, what was he doing there in the first place?"

"That's a good question. I don't think he got there by boat. It's too treacherous to land anywhere near there. He must have walked in." Morgan felt a chill run up her spine thinking of a random stranger walking around in their yard while they slept.

"Well, maybe we'll get some answers once we find out who the guy was and why he was killed. Until then, there's not much we can do except work."

Fiona turned her attention back to the necklace. Morgan looked at the stack of orders she had for herbal mixtures. Picking one from the top she gathered various herbs from her stock, placing small amounts into a stone mortar for grinding.

The girls worked in silence and time passed slowly, measured by the ticking of the grandfather clock in the back of the store.

Morgan was almost in a trance, grinding together a mixture of ginger, black horehound, raspberry leaf and mint for a seasickness remedy when the bell over the shop door announced a customer.

"Hello girls!" Amelia Budding, one of their elderly regulars, shuffled into the shop, her magenta polyester shirt and shorts somehow made her four foot frame seem even smaller.

"Hey, Amelia." Fiona put down the moonstone cabochon she was working with and stood up. "What can we do for you?"

"Oh I'm looking for some black onyx, you know, to protect myself in case evil descends on the town." Amelia shuffled toward Fiona's antique oak jewelry display case, which she was barely tall enough to look down into.

Morgan and Fiona exchanged raised eyebrow looks over her head.

"Evil?" Morgan ventured.

"Well, I heard about the trouble out at your place."

"And you think some evil menace is involved?" Fiona bent down on the other side of the case and removed a black bracelet.

"Well, I heard tell it might have something to do with pirates ... and you know how nasty they can be."

"Pirates? I thought they died out two hundred years ago?" Morgan narrowed her eyes at Amelia. *Surely the woman couldn't be serious?*

Amelia shrugged and looked across the room at Morgan over the tops of her eyeglasses. "Believe what you want. If you're great-grandma were alive she'd have some tales to tell you."

The girls exchanged another look. Morgan was three years older than Fiona and only had the vaguest of memories of their great-grandmother. She wasn't even sure if they were real memories or just from pictures and stories she'd been told. She didn't remember anything about pirates in those stories.

Fiona laid the black bracelet on a purple velvet cushion. "This one is all black onyx with a sterling silver clasp." She unhooked the bracelet, laying it over her wrist to demonstrate how it would look.

"And black onyx will protect me, right?"

"That's one of its powers. It will also make you stronger and alleviate worry," Fiona said then raised her head to look at Morgan. "And it can also help you let go of past relationships and move on with your life."

Morgan ignored the pointed look from her sister. Since Fiona had gotten involved with Jake, she'd been on a mission to get Morgan to forget about Luke and find someone new. It's not like Morgan didn't *want* to. She glanced over at the jewelry case warily. Maybe she *should* consider wearing some black onyx.

"It's perfect." Amelia unsnapped her purse and dug out an overstuffed wallet, squinting into it as she retrieved some bills.

Fiona rang up the sale and they watched Amelia shuffle toward the door. Just as she reached for the handle, she turned back dramatically, pointing her bespectacled gaze at Fiona and then Morgan.

"You girls be careful now. I think dangerous times are upon us," she said, then opened the door and shuffled out.

"Is she for real?" Morgan squinted at the door then looked at Fiona.

"Pirates? Seriously? I don't think so." Fiona laughed. "She's almost one hundred years old for crying out loud. She's probably senile."

Morgan laughed. "Yeah, she's probably just inventing danger to make her life more interesting.

After all, what else is there to do when you get to be in your nineties?"

"Right. I'm sure there's a logical explanation for the body on the cliff that has nothing to do with pirates or some evil menace that's going to descend on the town."

"Of course, that would be ridiculous," Morgan agreed. But, as she turned back to her work, she had to wonder—if it was so ridiculous, why did she have that nagging feeling of doom in the pit of her stomach.

3

Luke stared at Morgan through his high powered binoculars. She was even more beautiful than he remembered.

He was glad to see she still had that long ebony hair he'd found so appealing. His pulse quickened as he remembered the silky feel of it in his hands. And even though he couldn't see them, his heart clenched remembering her ice-blue eyes that could make him melt with a single look.

He put the binoculars down with a sigh. He was better off not remembering. He'd chosen the military over her. It really wasn't a decision he had much control over—it was more of a calling he couldn't ignore … to do his part for the country.

He didn't think it was fair to expect her to wait for him. What if he got maimed or killed in action? He'd loved her too much to put her through that, so he'd broken things off. It had nearly killed him to do it, but he felt she deserved a chance to find someone who could be there for her. His gut churned as he wondered if she'd found that someone.

Seeing her after all these years stirred up feelings that he hadn't had in a long time. Feelings that he thought were dead and buried … feelings that he had no time for now.

Luke used his Special Forces training to shut off his thoughts. It wouldn't do him any good to start pining over something he couldn't have.

True, he was no longer in the Special Forces. Now he had a different job. A more dangerous job. That was why he had to push aside his longing to see Morgan. He'd do everything he could to protect her while he insured the success of the job he had come here for, but he had to do that all from afar.

He was afraid of what might happen if he let himself talk to Morgan. Afraid of his feelings, and also of what he might tell her. Morgan always had a way of getting him to spill his guts and he knew he wouldn't be able to lie to her.

He picked up his binoculars and scanned the forest while pushing all thoughts of Morgan from his mind. The sooner he forgot about their past relationship, the better. He'd have to take care to keep his distance. Her safety and the success of his mission depended on it.

No matter how much he wanted to talk to her, Morgan Blackmoore was off limits—he couldn't take any chances on her discovering the secret of why he was really back in town.

4

"What do you mean you can't find anything on him? Can't you trace him by his fingerprints or dental records or something?" Morgan looked across the table at Jake as she took a sip from her beer bottle.

"Only if they have records on file. This guy apparently didn't. And he had no ID on him so ..." Jake bent down to scratch Belladonna who had flopped down adoringly at his feet.

"Surely, you guys must have other ways of identifying a body?" Fiona asked.

"Well, the Noquitt P.D. isn't exactly on the cutting edge of technology and Overton seems to be dragging his feet with this one." Jake creased his brow. "For some strange reason, he's not really putting a big effort into figuring out who this guy is."

Morgan glanced across their yard at the crisp, blue Atlantic Ocean, her eyes falling on the section of cliff still marred by yellow police tape. She wondered why Overton wouldn't be pulling out all the stops to find the identity of the man who died there. She could think of only one reason—he knew something they didn't.

"Anyway, he's keeping me as far from the case as he possibly can." Jake's words pulled Morgan's attention back to the patio table on the edge of their backyard where she sat with Jake and her sisters. Even though Jake and Fiona had tried to keep their relationship a secret from the sheriff, this was a small town and everyone knew everyone else's business. Morgan figured Overton probably had it in for Jake now, too.

She looked at the beer bottle in front of her, condensation running down the sides created a puddle on the table. The evening sun was low in the sky and the day had cooled slightly, but it was still hot and humid—a typical Maine summer night.

She took a deep breath of salty ocean air mingled with the smell of fried clams and drained the rest of her beer. Grabbing another one from the cooler, she picked nervously at the edge of the label.

"Was he murdered?" Morgan asked.

Jake shrugged. "All I could find out was that he was killed by a blow to the head. He might have fallen and cracked his head on the rock, but he would have had to have fallen pretty hard for it to be fatal."

"Is Overton going to try to blame us somehow?" Celeste asked from the edge of the patio where she had been watering the colorful flowers they had set in large pots and containers.

Jake ran his hands through his short cropped hair. "I think he'd like to, but without knowing who the guy is, he can't come up with a plausible motive. Although I did hear him mention that you all had means and opportunity."

"Well, that's crazy. It doesn't have anything to do with us!" Fiona's blue eyes sparked with anger.

"I'm not so sure," Morgan said handing Fiona a beer. "I mean, I know none of us killed him, but I'm not so sure his being on our cliff had nothing to do with us. I have a funny feeling about this."

Celeste joined them at the table. "Oh, that's right —Nana wanted me to tell you that you should trust your feelings, Morgan."

Everyone's head swiveled in Celeste's direction, even Jolene who'd had her head buried in her smartphone the whole time they'd been sitting there.

"What?" A tingle ran up Morgan's spine and she narrowed her eyes at her sister.

Celeste shrugged. "When I meditate, sometimes she comes and talks to me. It's nothing unusual."

"Sounds pretty unusual to me, Nana's been dead for ten years." Jolene lifted her sunglasses to stare at Celeste.

Fiona and Jake stared at her as if she'd announced she could walk on water, but Morgan noticed that didn't seem to faze Celeste at all.

Celeste had always been spiritually minded and Morgan knew she took her yoga and meditation seriously. But she'd never heard Celeste mention anything about talking to dead people before. Morgan didn't know what to think. She wasn't sure she actually believed in any of that stuff, but Celeste had never been one to act all "woo woo". Anyway, she had more important things to worry about right now.

"And what about that black hand thing?" Celeste was saying, "I feel like that might be some kind of clue, don't you, Morgan?"

Morgan wrinkled her brow. The black mark was odd. She had no idea what it meant, but it was the only thing they had to go on at this point.

"Black hand thing?" Jolene shifted her gaze between Morgan and Celeste.

"Yeah, the victim had a round black mark on his hand. Kind of like a tattoo."

Jolene raised her eyebrows and picked up her smartphone. "Maybe we can find something on the internet about that."

Morgan leaned back in her chair. They'd discovered a few months ago that Jolene was something of a whiz with computers when she'd uncovered some vital information that led them to find the real killer of Prudence Littlefield and clear Morgan's name. Morgan's chest swelled with pride, especially since they had been worried that Jolene might not find any positive direction in life given some of her shenanigans in high school.

She'd matured a lot since she had graduated and was even taking a computer forensics class during the summer. Maybe she'd have a career in law enforcement? God knows Morgan could use her help given the trouble Overton seemed hell bent on causing them.

Jolene's laughter pulled her out of her thoughts. "Did you find something?"

"Not hardly. The only thing I can find is that pirates use a black mark to indicate doom or death. If a pirate is marked with it, his days are numbered." Jolene looked up at Morgan, a smirk on her face. "Isn't that ridiculous?"

Morgan's heart jerked in her chest and she looked up at Fiona who was staring back at her wide-eyed. Amelia Budding's warning about pirates and evil echoed in her head.

Jolene's brow creased. "What? That's silly, right? There's no such thing as pirates anymore."

Morgan was about to answer when Belladonna leapt up on the table, let out a screech and then ran off into the bushes on the side of the house. Everyone jumped back, their chairs scraping on the patio, beers spilling on the table.

Morgan blotted beer from the crotch of her jeans, staring in the direction of the disappearing cat.

An icy tingle crept up her spine at the cat's unlikely timing. It was almost as if she had reacted to the discussion of pirates. Morgan laughed at herself. That was ridiculous, Belladonna didn't have uncanny powers and the days of pirates died out long ago.

But at this point she couldn't afford to ignore any clues no matter how silly they seemed. And since she didn't have much else to go on, it might be worth her while to learn a little bit more about pirates. Luckily she knew exactly the right person to help her.

5

The day was heating up to be a scorcher, Morgan thought, as she and Celeste walked down Maine Street toward *Reed Pawn and Antiques*. The pawn shop was located in the city, about twenty miles from their small town, and Morgan didn't come to the city too often.

They'd taken her car because Celeste's was loaded with yoga mats and various pieces of odd looking exercise equipment, including her latest obsession—kettle bells. Morgan had forgotten how busy and crowded it could be and how hard it would be to find a parking spot.

"I'm glad we parked a few blocks away, the morning is gorgeous, and it's not too hot yet." Celeste echoed her thoughts.

"Yeah, I can use the exercise after those beers last

night." Morgan looked down at her slim hips and stomach. *Were they getting bigger, or was it just her imagination?* Maybe she should cut back on the beer and ice cream.

The girls stopped in front of the upscale pawn shop, owned by their childhood friend Cal Reed. Cal was a history buff and antique expert—if anyone could tell them about pirates, it was him.

Celeste held the door open and a blast of cold air hit Morgan as soon as she stepped over the threshold.

"Brrr … It's freezing in here." Morgan rubbed her bare shoulders wishing she'd brought a sweater.

"Well, if it isn't my favorite girls!" Cal stood behind the glass display case, a genuine smile highlighted the dimples on his handsome face.

Just seeing Cal always cheered Morgan up. They'd been friends since they were kids and he was a frequent visitor to the Blackmoore house. He was practically like a brother to them, which probably explained why he'd never dated any of them. Cal was considered one of the most charming, handsome and eligible bachelors in the county, and literally had women swooning at his feet.

He was well known for being a playboy, but he was also a really nice guy and Morgan was glad he hadn't ruined the special friendship he had with the

Blackmoore girls by getting romantically involved with any of them. Cal's romances never lasted very long.

"What brings you guys here?" He asked, coming out from behind the case to envelop them both in a big hug.

"We need a history lesson," Celeste said.

Cal raised an eyebrow and looked from Celeste to Morgan. "About what?"

"Pirates," Morgan offered.

"Pirates?" Cal cocked an eyebrow at Morgan. "What's going on?"

"Well, you heard about the guy on our cliff, right?" Celeste ventured.

"What? No. I just got back from Barbados." Cal stared at her, concern clouding his deep blue eyes. "What guy?"

Morgan sighed. "A guy ended up dead on the cliff in our backyard. I discovered him yesterday morning."

"How did he die?" Cal alternated his gaze between Morgan and Celeste. "What was he doing on the cliff?"

"That's what we're trying to figure out," Celeste said.

"And you have no idea who he is?"

"Nope and Overton can't seem to figure it out either."

Cal snorted. "I'm not surprised. Overton's an idiot. It's a miracle he can find his way to the police station every morning. No wonder you guys have to investigate it on your own." He rubbed his chin then narrowed his eyes at Morgan. "But how do pirates figure into it?"

"The only clue we have is that the guy had a large black circle on his hand. Jolene looked it up and it's supposed to be some kind of pirate sign of doom or something." Morgan laughed. "I know it's silly. There's no such thing as pirates anymore, but we figure it was worth talking about. Maybe it will tie in to something useful … and we always like to have an excuse to come and talk to you."

"Aww, you guys know you don't need an excuse to see me. But the pirate angle might not be as farfetched as you think." Cal leaned back against the display case.

"Really?" Morgan's brow creased, her stomach fluttering.

"Well, there *are* modern day pirates, but I don't think that would tie into your dead guy. Modern pirates hijack cargo ships and steal the goods or hold them for ransom. But they don't do that around here." Cal walked over to one of the bookshelves that lined the store and pulled out a thick leather bound book, then leafed through it. "The black mark really is a pirate warning. I believe it's mostly fictional though. It was used to mark a pirate for death—a warning of sorts."

"Well, the guy on the cliff sure did end up dead," Celeste said looking over Cal's shoulder at the page of the book he was holding open.

"I still don't get what that has to do with us," Morgan said.

"It might not have anything to do with you, but it could be that the guy thought your cliff was a likely place for pirates to have buried their treasure."

Morgan laughed. "What? They only did that in the Caribbean. There's no pirate treasure around here."

Cal shook his head. "Legend has it many pirates buried treasure all over the Maine coast. The most Famous is Capt. William Kidd, but there were others. In fact, a cache of gold and silver Spanish coins were dug up just over in Biddeford, in the 1930s that many believe was buried there by pirates."

Morgan felt her eyes grow wider. "Seriously? But, why our cliff?"

Cal shrugged. "Who knows? I do know there are

people who make a living out of trying to find this type of treasure. Maybe someone's research led them to your location."

Morgan looked at Celeste. "Boy, finding a chest full of pirate treasure would sure solve all our money problems."

Morgan and Fiona made a modest living with *Sticks and Stones* and Celeste did fairly well with her yoga studio, but it was barely enough to put food on the table and pay the taxes on their property—which for a waterfront mansion was a small fortune. The house had been built generations ago so, luckily, they had no mortgage. Otherwise they wouldn't be able to afford to keep the house.

Celeste laughed. "Yeah, I'm sure there's a bunch of pirate treasure just buried all over our yard and no one found it in the three hundred some odd years people have been living there."

"So who are these people that search for treasure. Do you mean like that guy who has the boat that looks for old shipwrecks?" Morgan rubbed her forehead. *What was that guy's name?* She snapped her fingers. "Ballard."

"Sort of. Except these guys aren't nearly as nice. Ballard is legit. The guys I am talking about do it under the radar. They want to steal the treasure and keep all of it, without paying taxes or giving any to the rightful owners it was originally stolen from. And they'll do whatever they have to do to keep from getting caught." Cal's blue eyes drilled into Morgan's. "They are very dangerous people."

Morgan felt her stomach clench. "But he's dead now, so we probably don't have to worry, right?"

Cal shook his head. "I wish. But they usually travel in groups. There are probably others and if that guy thought your property had treasure, then the others might too."

Morgan and Celeste exchanged worried glances.

"When was your house built?" Cal asked.

Morgan wrinkled her brow and looked at Celeste uncertainly. "I don't know, sometime in the early 1700s I think. At least that's when the first part was built and then they added to it over the years."

"Did your family own the land before that? There were pirates back in that time ... maybe ..."

"You don't really think there would be pirate treasure there do you?"

"You never know." Cal shrugged. "What did you say your ancestor that build the house did for a living?"

"He was a merchant," Celeste said then her eyes went wide. "A sailing merchant."

Cal raised his eyebrows. "Didn't you guys find some old journals of his in your attic?"

"We found old journals, but we're not sure what year they are from," Celeste said. "They did look very old, but I don't know if they could be 300 years old."

"Well, maybe it's worth going up there and taking a look. Who knows? You might find an old treasure map or something." Cal winked at Morgan.

"A treasure map would be great." Morgan laughed, "but even if he was there looking for treasure, which I highly doubt, how did he end up dead?"

"Well, you said he had that black mark on his hand. Legend has it that when a pirate woke up with that mark on his hand, he'd better watch out because it meant he was marked for death. And that's exactly what happened to him." Cal wiggled his eyebrows at Morgan and Celeste. "So you see, it makes perfect sense."

"Pfft." Morgan waved her hand in the air. "I'm sure there's a logical explanation for all of it. There has to be, because believing a pirate ended up dead on our cliff because of some old curse is just too crazy for anyone to believe … even me."

6

"All this pirate stuff is nonsense, don't you think?" Morgan asked as they left the pawn shop and headed down the sidewalk.

"It is rather fanciful, but anything is possible, Morgan."

Morgan sighed. Leave it to Celeste to believe in something like pirates and curses.

"Hey, you wanna stop in at *Riley's* for lunch?" Morgan glanced at her watch. "Fi isn't expecting me back at *Sticks and Stones* until noon and all this pirate talk made me hungry."

"Sure. I love their veggie burgers."

They took a right down the side street that was a shortcut to *Riley's*—one of the city's most popular burger places. The route wasn't the most scenic and would take them through an undesirable section of town, but it cut a half mile out of the walk so it was a good trade off.

An uneasy feeling came over Morgan as they walked—like a heavy feeling of doom deep in the pit of her stomach. *Probably all this pirate talk has me unsettled.* She tried pushing the feeling away, but it insisted on staying like an unwanted houseguest that won't leave no matter how many hints you give them.

"… dying to read more of that journal," Celeste was saying.

"What?" Morgan asked, the strange feeling deepening as they turned down an out of the way street that housed a few abandoned buildings.

"I was saying, ever since we discovered that journal in the attic, I've been dying to get back up there and try to figure out what it says." Celeste stopped in her tracks her face a mask of concern. "Is something wrong?"

"No." Morgan shook her head. "This street just kind of gives me the creeps."

Morgan's thoughts drifted to the journal they had found in the attic as the girls walked a little faster down the street. None of them ever went in the attic. Ever. Their mother had told them it was off limits when they were little girls and the threat had carried over into adulthood. None of them wanted to go in there—the place creeped Morgan out and she was sure her sisters felt the same way.

But when Morgan had been arrested for Prudence Littlefield's murder, earlier that summer, Fiona had been forced to go up there in the hopes she could find something of value to hire a lawyer. After all, the place was loaded with several generations of Blackmoore family "stuff" so there was bound to be something of value.

And that's when they'd found the journal. An old, handwritten leather bound book, tucked in a book-shelf. Celeste had tried to make sense of it, but the writing was old and faded. They hadn't been back up there since.

Morgan's thoughts were interrupted by a prickly sensation running through her body. Like a current of electricity that started deep in the pit of her stomach and put her senses on edge. It was like her usual "gut feeling" times twenty.

Morgan's attention was drawn to a narrow alley that opened up onto the street about ten feet ahead of them. She could feel the hairs on the back of her neck stand up and she had an overwhelming urge to run back in the direction they had come from. She glanced down the street in either direction. It was empty. No one would run to their rescue or hear them scream.

This is silly. She tried to push her feelings away, but they wouldn't budge.

Just as they approached the alley, Celeste's message from her grandmother echoed in her mind. *Trust your feelings.*

Morgan reacted without thinking. She pulled Celeste back just as a man lunged out from the alley. Her quick reaction caused him to just miss grabbing Celeste!

In a second Celeste crouched down and kicked her foot up, connecting with the guys jaw and sending him staggering backwards but not before a second man made a grab for her.

Morgan watched, amazed, as Celeste's elbow shot out into the man's face. She heard a crunch and saw a spray of blood. The man fell back into the alley holding his nose.

The first guy had recovered quickly and made a grab for Morgan while Celeste was giving the second guy a bloody nose. Morgan kicked out, connecting with his crotch and the man went down in a heap.

A noise in the alley across the street caught Morgan's attention. She saw men running toward them. The two men they'd been dealing with were rolling on the ground and she didn't feel like taking on anymore so she grabbed Celeste.

"Run!"

They ran back the way they had come, toward their car. Morgan glanced back over her shoulder and saw the men coming out of the alley weren't running for them, they went straight after the men that had attacked them. That didn't stop her from running though—her gut told her to get the hell out of there and, from now on, she was going to trust her feelings.

It wasn't until they were safely locked inside the car that Morgan realized one of the men who had come running out of the alley across from them looked an awful lot like Luke Hunter.

* * *

MORGAN GASPED for breath as her white knuckled fists clutched the steering wheel.

"Are you okay?" Celeste maneuvered her arm to inspect her elbow for damage. Morgan noticed her sister didn't seem nearly as out of breath as she was. Maybe she should take up yoga and kettle bells?

"Yeah. What was that all about?" Morgan twisted in her seat to look down the street. It looked like a normal sunny day in the city. People were window shopping casually. No one was coming after them. It was hard to believe they had just been attacked.

"Apparently those guys were meaning to grab us. For what, I don't know." Celeste shuddered visibly in her seat.

Morgan narrowed her eyes at her sister. "Where'd you learn to fight like that?"

"Oh, I take Karate and self-defense." Celeste turned concerned eyes on Morgan. "You might want to think about taking a class or two yourself, although you do have a mean crotch kick."

The girls giggled. Then Celeste turned serious.

"What made you grab me like that—at that very second?" Morgan saw Celeste's brow furrow.

"I trusted my feelings."

Celeste smiled. "So you did listen … and it's a good thing too, because if you hadn't pulled me back when you did, this whole incident might have had a different ending."

"Speaking of endings, did you see those guys that came running from the other alley?"

Celeste nodded.

"At first I thought they were after us, but I think they were trying to help us. Or at least they were going after the guys that tried to grab us."

Celeste turned to look out the back window. "Maybe we should go back and thank them?"

"I don't know. It's strange but one of those guys looked just like Luke Hunter." Morgan felt her stomach clench. *Could Luke be back in town?*

Celeste swiveled around to face Morgan. "Luke? What would he be doing here? Besides, wouldn't he contact you if he was back in town?"

Morgan's heart tightened in her chest. "I don't know. We broke up almost ten years ago, so he certainly doesn't have to tell me where he goes. Besides he's probably married with kids by now."

"I thought he was still in the military?"

Morgan shrugged. "Yeah, it was probably just someone who looked like him."

"Didn't you see someone you thought looked like him a couple of weeks ago?" Celeste raised a brow at Morgan. "I think maybe you need to start dating again."

Morgan laughed as she started up the car. "Yeah, you can say that again."

"Do you think we should tell the cops?"

Morgan bit her lower lip. Given her experiences with Overton, she didn't have much confidence in the police. "Nah. We're not hurt and I'm sure those thugs are gone by now. What would the police do?"

"Yeah, I guess there's not much they can do. Do you think this has something to do with the guy on the cliff?"

Morgan's stomach churned. *Did it?* "No. How could it? I mean we're not even near home. That was probably just a couple of thugs who were waiting around to mug the next person that walked down the street."

"Yeah, probably." Celeste looked in the side view mirror uncertainly.

"But, let's not tell Fiona or Jolene. I don't want them to get all worried."

"Okay," Celeste agreed.

Morgan eased out of the parking spot, glancing nervously behind her one last time.

Did she really believe it was just a random mugging?

Her logical brain told her it was, but her gut was telling her something else entirely. And, if her gut instincts were right, she'd have to find out who the dead guy was, and what he wanted, quickly ... before something worse happened.

MORGAN SIPPED a steaming cup of chamomile and valerian tea to calm her nerves as she sat at her worktable at *Sticks and Stones* and filled Fiona in on the meeting with Cal.

"Do you really think he was after some sort of treasure?" Fiona looked at Morgan with wide blue eyes.

"No. Don't you think if our family had a treasure we'd know about it?"

"Maybe it was buried there before any Black-moores got here. You did say that pirates were rumored to bury treasure all up and down the coast, right?"

"Yeah, but that's reaching pretty far to think treasure could be on our land."

"Well, if it is, I want *us* to find it, not some treasure hunters."

Morgan laughed. "Me too. But even if that *was* why he was there, it doesn't explain why he ended up dead."

"True. Well, maybe it was just one of those things and we'll never hear anything about it again."

"I wish," Morgan said looking out the front window of *Sticks and Stones* where she could see Sheriff Overton's car pulling up to the shop. She watched him get out, hitch up his pants and stomp to the door which he yanked open, then stood in the opening silhouetted in the sunlight.

"Good afternoon, Sheriff. Come on in," Morgan said with feigned cheerfulness.

Overton glared in her direction, stepped inside and shut the door.

"What brings *you* here?" Fiona stood up from her workbench and narrowed her eyes at Overton.

"I have some questions for you girls. You can answer them here or I can take you down to the station."

Morgan shot Fiona a warning glance and shrugged. "We can answer them here."

Overton looked disappointed. He switched the toothpick from the right side of his mouth to the left and leaned back on his heels.

"Alrighty, then." He pulled a notebook and pencil out of his pocket and licked the tip of the pencil causing Fiona to make a face. "How long did you know the deceased?"

"Huh? You mean the man I found on the cliff?" Morgan's brows mashed together. "We didn't know him at all."

Overton looked at her from under his shaggy eyebrows. "Really? You expect me to believe that?"

"It's the truth." Morgan struggled to remain calm. She knew Overton was looking for them to overreact. He was probably trying to incite them, hoping they'd do something crazy so he could arrest them. She refused to play his game.

"Well, now how could a big man like that walk all the way past your house and out onto the cliff without anyone noticing?"

Morgan's stomach clenched. She'd been wondering the same thing. "He must have snuck out there in the middle of the night."

Overton cocked an eyebrow at her. "Now why would someone do that?"

"We have no idea. Are you accusing us of something?" Fiona cut in from across the room.

Overton smirked at her. "Not yet. But I know you girls are involved somehow."

Morgan drew in a deep breath. "Really Sheriff, we're not involved in every crime that happens in this town."

Overton turned to Morgan, the toothpick wiggling back and forth as he talked. "With your track record and the fact the deceased was found on your property, I'm sure it's only a matter of time before I'm able to charge you with something."

Morgan walked over to the door and held it open, gesturing for Overton to leave.

"I doubt that. You won't find anything relating us to that guy's murder because *we didn't have anything to do with it.*" She punctuated the last words by leaning forward, almost in his face.

Morgan felt a wave of triumph when Overton started to leave, but the triumph was soon replaced with a twinge of worry when she saw the satisfied smirk on his face.

He turned just inside the doorway and his words caused Morgan's stomach to twist into a knot.

"Oh really? Then why did we find a copy of the *Ocean's Revenge* ship's manifest from 1722 showing Isaiah Blackmoore as the captain in his pocket?"

7

Celeste sat cross legged on the floor of the Library. She always meditated in this room—it was her favorite. She loved the dusty smell of antique furniture and old leather books and the way the sun spilled in through the nine foot tall windows highlighting rich colored slices of the antique Persian rugs.

She didn't know if it was the hand carved oak bookcases or the centuries old leather couches and chairs or the gigantic marble fireplace, but somehow, the room felt both awe inspiring and cozy at the same time.

The room also seemed spiritual somehow. Maybe because of all the old books and furniture that were once read and used by ancestors long dead, or maybe because it was so quiet—especially now when no one else was home.

She settled herself in a patch of sun and closed her eyes, breathing slowly in through her nose and out through her mouth. Slowly in … and slowly out.

She cleared all thoughts from her mind. Every time a conscious thought tried to invade she dismissed it, promising her conscious mind she would deal with it later. Slowly, she counted backwards, clearing her mind of any thoughts that tugged at it, waiting for her subconscious to take over.

She could feel herself drift off … still conscious, but not really. It was almost as if she could go to some other land inside her mind. She was getting better at entering this special land the more she meditated. It was coming to her faster and faster. And now she was even hearing the voices.

At first she could only hear a few whispered words from her spirit guide, Andrew. But that gradually progressed to full conversations and the past few times she'd meditated she'd also talked to her grandmother. At first it had freaked her out a little, but now she was starting to look forward to her meditations and these little visits from the other side.

"Well, don't you think you should be up in the attic looking for that book?"

Celeste jumped at her grandmother's voice. She'd heard it before, of course, but this time instead of being inside her head, it sounded like it was right in the room beside her.

Celeste focused on thinking up a response in her head.

I'm not sure. My sisters don't seem too keen on going up there.

"Nonsense, why not? There's lots of neat family stuff up there. And, of course, the journals."

Mom always told us to stay away, is it okay with her?

"How would I know?"

Isn't she there with you?

"No."

Celeste felt her brows knit together. Her mother had died four years ago, if she wasn't "over there" with Nana, then where was she? She found herself wishing she could see her grandmother and not just hear her disembodied voice in her thoughts.

"Well, why don't you just open your eyes if you want to see me?"

Celeste's heart skipped a beat. *See her?*

She tentatively cracked open one eyelid. She didn't see her Nana. She did see Belladonna, though. The cat was over by the window swatting at the haze that drifted in from the late afternoon sun. No, wait, it was more of a mist … and the mist was bending down to pet the cat.

Celeste opened her other eye and watched open-mouthed as the cat rolled over on her back, the mist taking the shape of a human, bending over, its arm extended toward the cat and rubbing her belly.

The mist stood up and turned to her. "See dear, you can see me *and* hear me."

Celeste squinted. The figure was fuzzy, but she could just make out some of her grandmother's features. Her eyeglasses, and her hair in a bun on top of her head. She was even wearing an apron that Celeste remembered from her childhood, or at least that she'd seen Nana wearing in pictures.

Celeste stared at the apparition, speechless.

"What's a matter, cat got your tongue?" Nana laughed and Belladonna let out a meow.

Celeste wondered if she'd fallen asleep and was dreaming.

The misty figure looked at its watch. "Well, I've gotta run, but I wanted to put a bee in your bonnet about the attic. There's important stuff up there you girls are going to need."

"Okay," Celeste stammered.

"Well, then, ta-ta." Nana bent to scratch

Belladonna behind the ears and then vanished in a misty swirl.

Celeste sat still for a few minutes, her heart pounding against her ribs. *Did that really just happen?*

Belladonna came over and rubbed herself against Celeste's legs. She scratched the cat's head in return.

"Mew." Belladonna flopped down on her side and aimed her ice-blue eyes at Celeste then flicked them up towards the ceiling … where the attic was.

She heard the front door open and glanced at the green onyx art deco clock on the mantel. It was five thirty, which meant it must be Morgan and Fiona coming home.

Celeste took a deep breath and stood up on shaky legs. All indications pointed toward the attic and if that's where the powers that be wanted her to go, then who was she to argue?

She just hoped she would have as easy a time convincing her sisters of that as her grandmother'd had convincing her.

MORGAN SHUT the front door and proceeded down the hall toward the kitchen, her heart skittering when she saw a pale and shaken Celeste coming out of the library.

"What's the matter? You look like you've seen a ghost?" Morgan wrinkled her brow in concern as she studied her sister's face.

"Oh." Celeste ran her fingers through her perky blonde hair. "Sorry, I was napping and I'm still half asleep, I guess."

Morgan put her arm around Celeste's shoulders and led her into the kitchen. "Come on. We'll make some supper and tell you all about our visit from Overton."

"Sheriff Overton? Oh no. Is he going to arrest one of us or something?"

"I'm sure he'd like to but, fortunately, he doesn't have any evidence. He did, however, let it slip that he found something very interesting on the dead guy."

The girls stepped into the spacious black and white tiled kitchen. The kitchen itself had been built during one of the many home renovations in the 1800s and still had the original dark wood cabinets which were offset by white marble counter tops. The stainless steel appliances were a newer addition to the kitchen as was the large island in the center.

The smell of shrimp, garlic and fresh herbs hit Morgan's nose, causing her mouth to water. Fiona turned from the stove and looked at them as they each took a seat at the island.

"So, what's this interesting thing that Overton told you about?" Celeste reminded Morgan.

"You won't believe it." Morgan felt her heart speed up with a flitter of excitement despite the logical part of her brain telling her this all had nothing to do with pirate treasure. "Overton said the guy had a copy of some sort of ship's manifest that one of our relatives was the captain of in his pocket!"

"What?" Celeste's eyes widened as she divided her attention between Morgan and Fiona.

"Yep," Fiona said, swirling the shrimp in the pan "Jake's going to see if he can snag a copy of it and bring it over for us to look at."

"So what does that mean, the guy really was looking for treasure?" Celeste asked.

"Maybe." Morgan got up and grabbed a large bowl of salad from the fridge, placing it on the island. "That doesn't mean there really *is* treasure, though."

"It will be kind of cool to see what sorts of things were on the ship of our great-great-great-great-great-great-grandfather though." Fiona poured the shrimp concoction over a bowl of pasta, tossed it together and set it on the island next to the salad.

"Are you sure that's enough 'greats'?" Morgan asked, grabbing plates from the cupboard.

Fiona laughed, waving her hand in the air. "Well, who knows how many, I know there's a lot. The guy lived over three hundred years ago."

Morgan filled her plate and sat at the island beside her sisters. She had a forkful of food halfway to her mouth when a knock sounded on the front door.

Fiona jumped up. "That must be Jake."

"I'm sure it is. He has an uncanny way of showing up just when the food is ready to eat," Morgan said good-naturedly. The truth was she adored Jake as did all the sisters.

Fiona ran off to open the door and Morgan used the opportunity to dig into her supper. She was almost done by the time Fiona ushered Jake into the kitchen.

"Did you get a copy?" Morgan asked, handing a plate to Jake.

"Yeah, I got one of the other cops to sneak me one. Overton is keeping me far away from the case. Putting me on crap jobs like traffic detail." Jake made a face as he dug in his pocket and pulled out a folded piece of paper.

He opened it and spread it on the island. The

three girls bent their heads over the paper to examine it.

"This is pretty cool," Celeste said. "The *Ocean's Revenge* ... I never heard of it but I like the name. Kind of sinister for a merchant ship though, don't you think?"

Morgan looked at the paper. The copy was blurry, the writing faint. She could see the original manifest itself had rough edges and many folds and creases. At the top was the date, ship's name and captain's name —Isaiah Blackmoore—below that columns with lists of items and numbers.

She ran her finger down the left column and read off the items. "Pottery, cowhide, turtle shell, cacao ... who knew they shipped this stuff around the world back then?"

"And who would care about recovering it now?" Celeste asked.

"Maybe not that stuff, but look at the bottom," Jake said between mouthfuls of shrimp.

Morgan skipped down to the bottom of the page and her heart jerked in her chest. "Gold and silver coins, copper ingots, silver bars ..." she looked up at her sisters. "Now *that's* worth recovering."

Fiona raised her brows. "For sure. But that was the stuff on his ship. It's not like he brought it home and buried it in the yard. He had to deliver that stuff to where ever it was supposed to go, didn't he?"

Morgan nodded. "And we don't even know if this is really an authentic ship's manifest."

"But it does give us a lead as to why the guy was on our cliff," Celeste said.

Morgan pursed her lips. "True, but not why he was killed."

"Do we even need to know that? I say it can't hurt to do a little treasure hunting ourselves. I mean, that guy certainly went to a lot of trouble to get killed on our cliff, maybe there is something to this whole buried treasure thing?" Fiona tore a piece of bread from the loaf on the table and used it to sop up what was left on her plate.

Jake looked up at them. "You might *have* to figure out why he was killed … or at least who killed him. Overton is all fired up about the manifest linking the dead guy to your family. I eavesdropped on one of his conversations and he was talking about getting a search warrant."

Morgan's stomach clenched. Someone had planted evidence in their yard to try to frame her for Prudence Littlefield's murder earlier in the summer and she suspected it was Overton.

"If he gets a search warrant, who knows what

kind of evidence he might plant. We can't let that happen."

Jake nodded. "You guys need to be careful, though. If that guy got killed looking for the treasure, it might be dangerous for *you* to look for it, not to mention how dangerous it would be to try to track down his killer."

Morgan's heart skipped a beat and she glanced over at Celeste, the memory of the guys who tried to grab them earlier that morning fresh in her head.

Celeste tapped her finger to her lips. "Either someone thinks this supposed treasure is worth killing over, or someone had a beef with this guy and just happened to kill him in our yard."

"Either way, I think we need to find out more about these treasure hunters. Maybe we can get Jolene to do some research online," Morgan said.

"I think we need to find out more about the *Ocean's Revenge*. If we can get a clue as to why this guy was interested in the ship we might uncover a motive for someone wanting to kill him," Celeste offered.

"And a motive could lead us to the killer," Jake added. "But be forewarned, you might find out your relative wasn't the honorable merchant you have been lead to believe."

The girls exchanged a look. *Was it possible their relative was some sort of pirate?*

"I think I know one way we can find out," Celeste said, glancing up at the ceiling toward the attic.

Morgan's stomach fluttered nervously as she followed Celeste's gaze. She never liked going up in the attic, but Celeste was right. If there were secrets to be uncovered about their ancestors, the attic was the place to find them.

8

"I say there's no time like the present," Fiona said, as she loaded the last of the dinner dishes into the dishwasher.

"To go in the attic?" Celeste asked.

"Why are you going in the attic?" Jolene appeared in the pantry doorway.

"Oh, there you are," Fiona said. "We just finished eating, are you hungry?"

"No, I ate at the restaurant."

Recently graduated from high school, Jolene had a summer job at *Barnacle Bill's*, a local restaurant, until she figured out what she wanted to do with her life. The side benefit was that she was fed well and often surprised them with some great take out.

"What's this about going in the attic?" She persisted.

Fiona glanced at Morgan. The two oldest sisters were used to sheltering Jolene from anything unpleasant, but Morgan figured Jolene was all grown up now and, if they wanted her to act like an adult, they should treat her like one. She nodded her head.

"We've got some more information on the dead guy Morgan found," Fiona said, then filled Jolene in about the pirate treasure hunters and the ship's manifest.

"We were hoping you could do some research online about these treasure hunter guys," Morgan added.

"Of course, whatever you guys need, just ask."

Celeste stood up, and started over toward the back stairs that led to the attic. "I'm heading up … who's coming?"

"Meoooow!" Belladonna streaked by her and ran up the stairs in a flash of white causing everyone in the room to laugh.

"Well, I guess one of us is excited," Morgan said as she followed behind Celeste.

The stairs, originally built for servants to travel from their quarters to the other floors without using the main staircase, were narrow. They ascended in single file amidst the groaning and creaking of the centuries old wood.

At each floor, the stairway opened up into a hallway for access—they went up four flights, each one seeming ten degrees warmer than the last.

By the time they got to the top, Morgan was breathing heavy. She bent over and put her hands on her knees. Sweat drenched her tee-shirt.

"Sheesh Celeste, you must be in good shape—you aren't winded at all," she said sucking in a deep breath and flapping the bottom of her shirt to let some air in.

Celeste smiled at her and Morgan smiled back despite the butterflies that were swarming in her stomach. The attic always made her feel this way. All that old stuff piled up with God knows what hiding behind it creeped her out.

Morgan looked around. It was dark out and the lighting in the attic wasn't that great—which made it even creepier. She suddenly had an image of them in old fashioned dresses, carrying torches and lanterns to light the way. She was glad they didn't have to resort to use torches … even though the image seemed quite real for a split second.

"Where was the book? Do you remember?"

Jake, Fiona and Jolene had caught up to them and the five of them stood in the doorway squinting into the attic. The space was immense, taking up the whole fourth floor and consisted of a main room with alcoves and other rooms beyond it. The stairs dumped them out into the main room which ran the width of the house and was just about as long as it was wide.

"It looks different up here now. Because there's not as much light, I suppose." Fiona stood on her tiptoes and swiveled her head around. "I think it was in that direction ... over by the window."

They picked their way through the various piles toward the window. The attic was crammed full of old furniture, trunks, rugs and boxes. Morgan could tell they were on the right path as she recognized some of the boxes they had opened on their trip up there earlier in the summer.

"That's it!" Celeste pointed to a bookcase near one of the dormer windows. Morgan wasn't surprised to find Belladonna sleeping right on top of it. The cat opened one eye lazily then closed it again.

Celeste carefully took the thick leather bound book out of the shelf and set it on a nearby table. She opened the cover, gently lifting the first page. Morgan held her breath, afraid the old paper might disintegrate into dust with each touch.

They gathered behind Celeste, peeking over her shoulder as she turned the yellowed pages.

"That looks like gibberish," Fiona said.

Morgan leaned closer, her brows creasing together, and tried to make sense of the writing. It had clearly been done with some sort of quill or fountain pen. The ink had faded almost to nothing and there were swirly flourishes and splotches that made it hard to make out the words.

"Can you understand any of this? The words are so strange."

"Well, they did have different words and spellings back then … but this seems like the words don't go together." Celeste leaned even closer.

"I think it might be some sort of code," Jolene said.

Everyone turned to her. "Code?"

"Yeah, you know like a secret message where you use code words and then have a key that tells you what the words mean."

Morgan felt her stomach sink. "Well, how the heck are we going to figure that out?"

"Maybe the key is around here somewhere." Fiona started poking in the bookcase. "Would it be a paper, or something else?"

"There could be a piece of paper that tells you how to decode it, but it's probably a code that he knew by heart, I doubt you would find anything here that's going to help you break the code," Jolene said.

Morgan felt her shoulder slump. "So we'll never know what it says?"

"There's some well-known codes that have been used for ages. You know, like replacing the letters of the alphabet with a number and so on. There were many ways people used to encode writing. We should find out some of the most common methods and see if they work on this book," Jake offered.

"I bet Cal will know about that," Celeste said, then looked at her watch. "It's too late to call him and I don't want to take the book anywhere—it's too fragile. Someone get me a paper and pen and I'll copy some of it down, then hook up with him tomorrow and see if he recognizes any of it."

Jolene scampered off and Morgan turned her attention to the rest of the room. It was filled with castoffs from previous generations. Family heirlooms … or junk? She wasn't sure which.

Over on the bookcase, Belladonna stretched lazily then jumped off and brushed past Morgan with a flick of her tail and a quick look over her shoulder. Morgan followed her. The cat weaved her way through the maze and Morgan trailed along, mesmerized by her ancestor's belongings that she passed along the way. A beautiful oak bureau with a marble top, a full length mirror with baroque gilt frame, an old playpen—Morgan wondered if it had been hers —and dozens of boxes and trunks.

Belladonna stopped at a small box and started sniffing. Morgan crouched down beside her and studied it. It was shaped like a miniature dome top trunk, about a foot long and four inches tall. It looked ancient.

Belladonna scratched at it and Morgan picked it up. It looked to be made from some sort of shiny hard, mottled substance. *Turtle shell?* Morgan felt a familiar tingle in her gut as she remembered the manifest from the *Ocean's Revenge*.

"Morgan? Where are you?"

Celeste's voice startled her and she looked around, noticing Jake and her sisters were rather far away on the other side of the attic. *Had she really strayed that far?*

"Oh, there you are. We're done here so we're heading back down. Are you going to stay up here alone?"

Morgan's heart jerked in her chest. *No way was she staying up here alone.*

"I'm coming," she said, then put the box back where she had found it and hurried to catch up to the rest of them.

9

"It's a gorgeous day today," Morgan said as she opened one of the back windows at *Sticks and Stones*. She poked her head out the window and inhaled the sharp, salty ocean air. The cottage was up on a cliff and set quite a ways in from the ocean, but she could still smell it as well as see the brilliant patch of blue sparkling through the trees.

"That it is." Fiona joined her at the window, her vanilla latte in hand. The woods behind the cottage were filled with old, thick trees and they watched the birds flitter between the branches, their chirps echoing through the forest. One tree, in particular was Morgan's favorite because someone had carved a heart with an "X" and two sets of initials in it generations ago—so long ago that the carving was now twenty feet high off the ground.

"Did you sleep good last night? I was up all night with nightmares about the attic." Fiona broke into her thoughts.

"Oh, I thought all that thrashing had something to do with Jake being in your room." Morgan teased her sister whose cheeks turned bright red. "But, to answer your question, I did sleep very well, surprisingly enough."

"Yeah, all this pirate stuff is a little disturbing," Fiona said as she headed back to her work table. "I mean what if the dead guy on the cliff isn't just some unrelated incident and more things are going to happen?"

Morgan thought back to the attack on her and Celeste the day before, but said nothing. *What good would it do to get Fiona more worried?*

"Well hopefully Jolene will be able to find something on those guys that hunt for treasure and that will give us a lead on the dead guy so we can put this all behind us," Morgan said, slipping in behind her work table.

"Yeah, Jake said he was getting off early today and he was going to get together with Jo and see what they could come up with. Hopefully they'll have some answers by the time we get home tonight."

Morgan nodded her agreement. The sooner

they got to the bottom of this, the better—that tingly feeling of being watched was getting to her. She was starting to feel like she was just waiting for the next attack, which made her all nervous and jumpy.

The bell on the shop door tingled and Anastasia LePage floated inside, her aqua and lime green caftan fluttering around her like a cloud.

"Girls, I need your help!"

Morgan raised her brow at the elderly, somewhat eccentric woman. One of their regular customers, Anastasia's quirky personality and repeat business had quickly made her one of Morgan's favorites.

"What do you need Anastasia?"

"Oh, I desperately need something for the gout. My big toe is all swollen and the pain is excruciating!"

She shoved her foot out from underneath her dress to illustrate. Morgan caught a glimpse of aqua rhinestone sandals and blue nail polish. Her toe did look a tad swollen.

"Oh, that looks painful," Morgan said. "Devils claw is good for gout. I think I have some in stock, would you like me to get you some?"

"Oh please dear, a big bag if you will."

Morgan turned to rummage through her shelves then said over her shoulder "Oh, and eat lots of tart cherries, and drink cherry juice … they'll help reduce the uric acid that causes gout."

"I'll have extra cherries in my cocktails, then." Anastasia winked at her.

"Labradorite can help with gout, too." Fiona held up an aqua and gray stone that glowed iridescent when the light hit it. "Wrap it in a bandage and put it right on the joint or use it in a foot bath. It can also help you have prophetic dreams if you sleep with it under your pillow."

Anastasia crossed over to Fiona and reached out for the gem. "It's so pretty. And I sure could use some dreams. If I can sleep at all that is—the lights from those damn boats were shining in my windows all night last night."

"Boats?" Fiona and Morgan asked at the same time.

"Yes, out near the entrance to Perkins Cove. On the ocean side of you girls' house. My cottage faces there and the lights glared right into my window. Woke me about two in the morning. Back and forth, back and forth … it went on for hours."

Morgan and Fiona exchanged a look. None of the boats went out at that time of night and they certainly didn't go back and forth in the mouth of the cove like Anastasia was describing. *Could the boats have something to do with everything that was going on?*

"I can give you some chamomile and valerian for sleeping if you want," Morgan offered.

"Oh, that would be lovely, I hope those boats aren't back again tonight."

"How many nights has this happened?"

"Just last night as far as I remember. Or if they were there previously it didn't wake me up. I'll take this lovely stone too." Anastasia handed the labradorite back to Fiona and the girls packaged up her purchases and sent her on her way.

Morgan looked at Fiona as soon as the door shut. "We have to find out more about those boats."

"Do you think it could have something to do with the dead guy?"

"Well it's certainly unusual. Have you ever heard of boats out at that time of night like that?"

"Nope, never. No lobsterman I know would be out in the dark."

"Right, I think I'll look into it after work. It could turn out to be the lead we've been waiting for."

10

M organ decided to stop down at Perkins Cove as soon as she got home to see if she could find out anything about the boats. If they had moored in the cove, the fishermen were sure to know about it.

Perkins Cove was a cluster of weathered buildings set on a finger of land that had the ocean on one side and an inlet on the other. Once old fisherman's shacks, they had been turned into quaint shops that sold everything from sweatshirts to jewelry to clam rolls. The shopping area was shaped in a horseshoe. The cove itself was on one side of the horseshoe and dotted with boats making a postcard perfect scene. There was a cluster of shops in the middle of the "U" and more shops on the other side which backed up to the Atlantic Ocean. A white, wooden self-serve drawbridge spanned across the narrowest part of the cove and tourists delighted in walking across it in the hopes a tall boat would come in and they could raise the bridge by pressing the button on one side.

The shopping area was small with about fourteen shops, but tourists loved it. The street, which was barely wide enough for one car, was usually packed with window shoppers. The Blackmoore house was just beyond the top of the horseshoe at the very peak of land that separated the cove from the ocean. Rather than try to find a parking spot, Morgan walked the short one eighth mile from her house.

The summer activity in the Cove always picked up her spirits. Happy tourists, kids eating ice cream, shoppers buying souvenirs and the smell of fried clams and seaweed made her smile as she made her way past the shops to the small parking lot reserved for fishermen that docked their boats in the Cove.

A couple of fishermen were gathered around the carcass of a giant tuna. Morgan joined them.

"Hi Brian, is that your catch?" Morgan asked a tall dark haired man, one of her high school classmates.

"Yep." Brian grinned with good reason, a tuna that size made for a nice pay day.

"Hey Morgan, heard you had some trouble over

at yer' place." This from Josiah Littlefield, an old weathered lobsterman Morgan had known since she was a little girl.

"Yeah, the guy on the cliff? Any of you know anything about him?" Morgan glanced around the group, but they all shook their heads.

"Have there been any new boats docking in the cove the past few nights?" She ventured.

More head shaking.

"Have you guys heard anything about any boats trolling the waters on the ocean side near the cove?" she raised her eyebrows at them.

"Are 'ya thinkin' that has somethin' to do with the body you found?" Josiah asked.

"Yeah, one of my customers at *Sticks and Stones* said she saw boats going back and forth near the mouth of the cove last night in the middle of the night. Who would do that?"

"No one here would." Brian looked around the group. "That's kind of crazy."

"I know, I was wondering if they moored the boats in the cove … whoever they are."

Morgan, Brian and Josiah turned to look at the boats stacked up in their moorings.

"Nope, nothin' but the usual boats in there," Josiah said.

"And you haven't heard about any strange boat activity?"

"Nope."

Morgan took a deep breath and blew it out. "Okay, well if you hear anything let me know. The police haven't been able to identify the deceased and it could be important."

"Sure'n we will."

Morgan turned back toward home, her stomach sinking. If the boats weren't moored in Perkins cove, then where were they?

* * *

MORGAN TRUDGED BACK to the house barely noticing the sights and smells of the cove. She was so occupied with her thoughts of how she could find out more about the boats that she almost didn't notice a movement to the left by the stand of trees that lined the cliff. Almost.

She jerked her head in that direction. *Was someone over there?* She stopped and squinted into the trees for a minute, but didn't see anyone. Continuing up the driveway, she chastised herself for being so jittery. It wasn't like her to get all jumpy over nothing.

Inside Fiona, Jake and Jolene were gathered

around Jolene's laptop in the informal living room, one of the smaller rooms in the twenty four room home. This room was Morgan's favorite. She found the gray and blue decor to be soothing and the view of the Atlantic Ocean from the large bay window stunning. The giant starfish, seashells and rustic painted furnishings with overstuffed cushions made it comfy and homey.

Fiona looked up at her as she entered the room. "Did they know anything about the boats?"

Morgan shook her head.

"What boats?" Jolene asked.

"One of our customers said she saw boats trolling around out there in the middle of the night." Morgan tilted her chin toward the ocean.

"Trolling around? What do you mean?"

"She said they were going back and forth in a pattern around 2 a.m. The lights woke her up," Fiona said.

"I think I might know why," Jake cut in and everyone looked in his direction.

"Jolene and I did a lot of research this afternoon and one of the things that treasure hunters can do to look for sunken treasure is to ping the bottom with sonar or boat-towed marine metal detectors. If those boats were going back and forth in a pattern, then that could have been what they were doing."

"And if it's the treasure stealers, then that would explain why they were doing it at two in the morning —they didn't want anyone to know," Jolene added.

Morgan glanced out the window at the Atlantic. *Had there been a sunken treasure just a stone's throw from their house all this time?*

"What else did you guys find out?" Morgan asked.

"Well, there really isn't much online about these treasure pirates. They're sort of an underground group. Well, actually, there are several groups. They get leads on where there might be some treasure and they try to go and steal it. They are very secretive because they don't want anyone to know what they are after, or even to know they have it once they get it." Jolene looked up at Morgan, her ice-blue eyes turning serious. "They're very dangerous people, so you better be careful if you plan to mess with them."

Morgan felt the funny feeling in the pit of her stomach intensify. "Well, it appears they think we have some treasure around here, so I don't see we have much choice."

"Yeah. If only we knew where it was—we could sure use the money ourselves. And if we found it first that might solve our problems with the treasure stealers *and* the tax office."

"I think we might be able to help with that," Celeste said from where she stood in the doorway with Cal.

"What do you mean?" Morgan raised an eyebrow in their direction.

"I showed Cal the code from the journal and he says it's something called a book cipher," Celeste said.

"Basically, the words in the journal indicate the chapter, verse and word in a second book. You use the second book, which is called the key, to decode what the journal says," Cal added.

"So we need the second book to decode it? How do we know which book it is?"

Cal ran his fingers through his hair. "Well, it would have to be a book that was as old as, or older than the journal. We need to look at the journal and see if it has a date, then try out any other books we can find that were published near that date. It's really a long shot that you'll have the key book here."

Morgan felt a spark of enthusiasm. Judging by the contents of the attic, her ancestors never threw *anything* away. There were a lot of books up there and she had a gut feeling the key book they needed was among them … and she was learning her gut feelings were usually right.

"Well, let's get a move on," she said heading for the stairs. "That journal could lead us to the treasure, and if there's a treasure out there from the *Ocean's Revenge* then it belongs to us. I don't know about you guys, but I'm not going to sit around doing nothing while some treasure stealing pirates take it right from under our noses!"

* * *

MORGAN SPRINTED up the stairs to the attic, the others close behind. They headed straight for the bookshelf where the journal was. No one was surprised to find Belladonna lying on top of it, watching them lazily.

"Let's see if this thing has a date," Celeste said taking the journal gently from the shelf.

Cal cringed when she opened it and leafed through the brittle pages. "You should think about wearing gloves when you handle that, the oils from your fingers could damage it."

"Oh." Celeste looked down at her fingers. "I didn't think about that."

"Lucky for you there's a pair right here." Fiona

picked a pair of white lace gloves from a pile of antique clothing and handed them to Celeste.

"Jeez, these are tiny," she said, stuffing her hands into the gloves.

Morgan got busy at the bookcase, pulling out anything that looked as ancient as the journal. Belladonna jumped off the shelf, twirled herself around Celeste's feet then meandered off toward the back of the room.

"This one looks pretty old." Morgan picked up a leather bound book that was falling apart at the spine and glanced at Celeste. She noticed her sister's fingers were poised over the book and she was looking toward the window, almost in a trance.

"Celeste?" Celeste nodded her head, but not at Morgan.

"Earth to Celeste," Fiona said from her position crouched on the other side of the bookcase.

"What? Oh. Sorry." She turned the pages in the book then pointed. "Here's the date, August 10, 1722."

"The same year as that ship's manifest." Morgan's heart beat a little faster.

Celeste turned ice-blue eyes on Morgan. "Yes, but the key book isn't in this bookshelf. It's back there."

She pointed toward the back of the room in the direction Belladonna had headed.

"Huh? How do you know that?" Jolene furrowed her brow at Celeste.

"Oh no. Not Nana again?" Fiona asked.

Celeste just smiled. "Let's just look back there, okay?"

Morgan shrugged and started toward the back.

"What's this about your Nana?" Cal asked.

"We'll fill you in later," Morgan said over her shoulder.

They stopped at a stack of books. She was half expecting Belladonna to be there, pointing at the book with her tail or something, but the cat was nowhere to be seen.

She looked through the stack. The top ones were canvas bound, the books toward the bottom of the stack had leather spines. She carefully moved the books off the top and handed the leather ones out to Fiona, Jolene, Jake and Cal. She took the last one for herself and Celeste bent over her shoulder.

"This one's dated 1795. Too new." Cal put the book down gently on the pile.

"This one is too," Jake said.

"This one is 1717." Jolene held up a book. The

binding was cracked and dusty, the pages thick and rough.

Cal took the book. "It's a poetry book. Perfect for a cipher key."

"Do you think that's the key?"

"It could be. We might as well try it, right?"

Morgan felt a tingle run through her veins. Finding a treasure would be cool, but would that help her find the killer?

She glanced out the attic window at the ocean. It had grown dark and the sea was black, the full moon's light sparkled on the caps of the waves. There were no boats out there. Yet.

"You guys go ahead and work on deciphering the book," Morgan said. "I'm going to keep a watch and see if those boats show up again. Maybe I can get a name or registration number. We still need to get a handle on the killer, and I have a funny feeling the closer we get to finding a treasure—if there even is one—the more dangerous it could be for us."

Morgan caught the look from Celeste. She almost certain the attack the other day wasn't a random mugging and from the look her sister was giving her, she felt the same way.

"And everyone please be careful." Morgan looked around.

These were the people she loved most in the world. Her heart ached at the thought of anything happening to one of them. "If the treasure pirates Jolene told us about are the ones who killed the guy on the cliff, and they're after pirate treasure on our land, then I'm pretty sure they won't think twice about killing one of us to get it."

11

Morgan jerked awake in the dark, her heart pounding against her ribs.

Was that a noise or a bad dream?

She glanced out the window of the turret room toward the Atlantic. No boats were out there. Looking at her watch, she saw it was 1:45.

And then she heard it again.

It came from the ground floor, smashing glass and loud voices. She was up from her seat in an instant and running downstairs.

She skidded into the living room at the same time as Fiona and Jake. It was pitch black and Morgan could only see shadowy figures. There was a fight going on, but she couldn't make out exactly who was fighting.

Someone grabbed her arm and she reached

behind her, grabbing a thick crystal vase she knew was on the sideboard. She swung it toward her assailant and was rewarded when they let go of her uttering a string of curse words.

The moonlight filtered in through the smashed side window and her eyes strained to adjust to the dark.

She could see men in dark clothing, some with ski masks. Surprisingly, it seemed like they were fighting each other.

How many people were in here?

She glanced around in time to see Celeste's blonde hair—one of the masked men was reaching for her!

"Celeste! Look out!" Morgan bolted across the room and launched herself at Celeste's assailant.

He went down in a heap on the floor, Morgan on top of him. She kicked at him as he tried to grab her. Out of the corner of her eye, she saw someone push over the china cabinet with a resounding crash. Broken glass and china spilled out all over the floor. Belladonna ran hissing from the room.

Someone grabbed her by the waist and pulled her back. She squirmed around, clawing at him, trying to get in a good position to inflict some damage but he was too strong.

Her heart raced as she kicked back, but her efforts only resounded in a muffled grunt and a tighter hold on her.

"Hey, I'm not going to hurt you … I'm here to help you."

Morgan froze in mid kick. She recognized that voice. Spinning around, she yanked off the mask.

Her heart jerked wildly in her chest when her eyes confirmed what her ears had already told her. The man holding her was her high school sweetheart, the man who had left her a decade ago—Luke Hunter.

She pushed away from him, hauled her arm back and slapped him across the face as hard as she could.

* * *

LUKE'S HAND flew up to his cheek. She still had a mean slap. He wasn't sure what stung more—his cheek or his heart. It wasn't exactly the greeting he'd been hoping for. He could hardly blame her, though. Showing up like this after all these years. She was sure to be mad at him.

"What are *you* doing here?" Morgan backed away from him and he stood where he was even though he ached to go after her.

"Like I said … I'm here to help you."

"What are you talking about, you broke into my house!" Morgan spread her arms to indicate the chaotic room. The lights had come on and Luke could see smashed glass, broken windows and five of his men dressed all in black wrestling two other men into handcuffs.

"We didn't break in." Luke nodded toward the two men being forced into the cuffs. "They did. We just followed them in so we could capture them."

The Blackmoore sisters huddled against the opposite wall staring at him with wide eyes.

"Luke Hunter?" Fiona's eyes darted from Luke to Morgan.

Luke spread his hands. "In the flesh."

"But what are you doing here? I thought you were in Afghanistan or something."

"I was. My tour ended and now I'm back. Well, for a little while." He glanced over at Morgan who was shooting daggers at him from her eyes.

"Luke is Morgan's … umm … he grew up here." Fiona turned to explain to a man who was standing with a protective arm around her. Luke wondered who he was but figured it wasn't the time for him to ask questions. He couldn't help but smile when he noticed there was no man with a protective arm around Morgan.

"So, what is he doing in your house in the middle of the night?" The man stepped forward.

"Yeah, what *are* you doing here?" Morgan stood with her hands on her hips looking ridiculously cute in pink pajamas with French poodles on them.

"And who are these other guys?" The blonde who Luke recognized as Celeste said. She had only been a teenager when he'd left and she'd grown into a beautiful woman. Not as beautiful as Morgan, though.

Luke rubbed his hands through his day old stubble. Morgan used to like that stubble. He found himself wondering if she still felt anything for him—then immediately pushed those thoughts aside. He was only in Noquitt to do a job and then his work would take him somewhere else, possibly to the other side of the world. This job didn't leave any room for relationships and he wished he hadn't had to let Morgan know he was here. He wished he'd never gotten this close to her—to touch her. But he had to in order to stop the guys that had broken in. And now that he had …

He let out a long breath, wondering how to explain just why he was there. He decided the simplest way was the best.

He nodded toward the handcuffed men who were

being dragged out. "Those men are after something they think you have, and my job is to stop them."

"What? So you're like some sort of secret police force?" Morgan's brow was all scrunched up.

"Sort of. Have you guys noticed anything strange going on?"

"Hell 'ya," a voice said from the other side of the room.

Luke's eyes widened when he realized the petite brunette must be Jolene. She'd only been around nine years old the last time he saw her, but she had those ice-blue eyes … the same as Morgan and all the Blackmoore sisters.

"First a dead guy shows up on the cliff. Then we start hearing stories about pirates and next thing you know we're getting broken into." She spread her arms to indicate the mess around them and Luke noticed she was bleeding.

"You're bleeding!" Fiona rushed over to the girl's side and took her arm, looking at the wound below the elbow.

Jolene looked down at her arm. "Ahh, that's not so bad."

"I'll get a bandage and some stuff to clean it off." Fiona rushed out of the room.

"Anyway, what exactly do *you* have to do with any of this?" Morgan stared him down.

"My company tracks down people that steal treasure and stops them."

"Your company? What kind of company is that? And just how do you find out where to track these people down?" The man that had been with Fiona narrowed his eyes at Luke and Luke figured he'd better make friends fast.

He put his hand out toward the guy. "I'm sorry, we haven't been introduced. I'm Luke Hunter."

The man reluctantly took his hand. "Jake Cooper."

Luke nodded. "Nice to meet you."

Jake's handshake was firm and the guy definitely had some muscles. He looked like he could take care of himself which was good. Luke might need his help protecting the Blackmoore girls if the shit hit the fan like he thought it was going to.

Fiona came back with some cotton swabs, alcohol, bandages and a big orange rock. Luke raised an eyebrow at the rock, but kept silent.

"Jake works on the Noquitt police force," Fiona said over her shoulder as she cleaned Jolene's arm and applied the bandage.

Luke raised his brows. "Oh? How do you like that?"

"It's okay."

Luke could tell by the look on Jake's face that he didn't like it much at all. Which was good, because Luke had a feeling Sheriff Overton wasn't to be trusted. And if Jake didn't get along with Overton that probably meant Jake *could* be trusted.

Everyone was silent for a moment, watching Fiona wrap Jolene's arm. It was a deep, nasty gash.

Fiona put the rock on the wound and wrapped gauze around it.

"Keep the stone wrapped close to it until we can get some herbs and medicines from the pharmacy. It should help you heal," Fiona said then, noticing everyone was looking at her with raised brows, she shrugged and added, "it's carnelian which is good for healing wounds. At least it can't hurt."

Everyone's attention was drawn toward the window where the men in black outfits were now nailing a large sheet of plywood in place.

"We'll get that glass replaced for you tomorrow … and clean up this mess," Luke said. "You guys might want to think about getting an alarm system."

"Can we move into the kitchen?" Fiona asked, "I could use some coffee. And, since Luke still hasn't fully explained himself, I think we're going to be up for a while."

The group moved into the kitchen. Luke noticed that Morgan kept her distance from him. He leaned against the counter while the others took positions standing and sitting around the island.

Fiona grabbed some mugs from the cabinet and popped a K-cup in the coffee maker.

"So Luke, you were saying ..." Celeste gestured for him to continue the explanation he'd started in the other room.

"Yes, tell us more about your company," Jake said. By the way Jake was studying him Luke knew it wasn't going to be easy to earn the other man's trust.

"The men that broke in here aren't nice people. They belong to a group of treasure hunters that scour the world for long lost treasure, and take it by any means they can. They're kind of like modern day pirates," Luke said. "The people that invest in my company pay me to get rid of them."

"We read up about them online. But why are they here?"

"They figure out where to go by digging into old documents and archives. As far as we can tell, they got a lead that there is treasure from an old ship here somewhere."

"Does this tie into the dead guy on the cliff?" Morgan asked.

"There are two groups of treasure hunters here in town. Rivals. One of the groups killed a member from the other group as a warning to back off."

Celeste's face brightened. "Well that's good to know, we can just tell Overton and he'll stop bothering us."

"Bothering you? About the murder?" Luke narrowed his eyes at Celeste.

"Yes, he seems to want to pin every murder in town on Morgan."

"*Every* murder?"

Morgan waved her hand. "I don't think Luke needs to know about all that."

Luke raised his brows at her.

"It's old news," she said. "But he did threaten us about the guy on the cliff. So tell us how to find these pirate guys and Jake can let him know they did the killing, and then Overton will leave us alone … at least about that, anyway."

"It might not be that simple. These guys hide out. It's not like they have an address or anything. They're practically invisible." Luke took a chance and said to Jake, "I'm not so sure Overton can be trusted to do the right thing. What do you think?"

Jake nodded, his stance relaxing a bit. "I agree. What makes you say that, though?"

"Just a feeling." Luke stared at Jake and he felt like he'd moved up a notch on the trust scale.

"Okay, so now that you have those guys." Jolene nodded toward the living room, "no one will be bothering us, right?"

"I wish it was that easy. Unfortunately, there are more where they came from."

"Sheesh, how many of these guys are there?" Fiona handed Luke a coffee.

"Quite a few. But I have quite a few guys too, and we're going keep a close eye on them … and on you, to make sure nothing more happens."

Morgan snorted. "I don't think you need to keep an eye on us, we're perfectly capable of taking care of ourselves … unless you're after the treasure too?"

Luke's heart clenched at the look of mistrust she gave him. "These guys are very dangerous and the fact that the two groups are in a fight for this treasure makes them even more so. You *do* need our help whether you want to admit it or not … and we're not after the treasure, we get paid very well by the people that hire us."

"I still don't understand what your job is or why

we should trust you," Morgan said. "Where did you take those men, anyway? To Overton?"

"No, not to Overton. We have ways of dealing with them that you don't need to know about. Just be glad there's two less that will be bothering you. And my job is to wipe out these scum—let's just say the people that pay me have a vested interest in getting rid of their kind and leave it at that."

He saw Morgan bite her bottom lip and knew he had his job cut out for him, getting her to trust him again.

"Now, the more you guys can tell me about this supposed treasure, the better I can help you."

Jolene looked up from her coffee mug. "The dead guy had a copy of a ship's manifest in his pocket from the ancestor that originally built this house. We tried to decipher one of his journals—"

"We're not sure the journals have anything to do with it," Morgan interrupted.

Luke raised an eyebrow. He knew they weren't telling him everything, but he hadn't expected them to right off the bat. "Well the more I know, the easier it will be for me to anticipate what the treasure hunters will do and the faster I'll be able to get rid of them."

He noticed Fiona, Jolene and Celeste flick their eyes over at Morgan and she shook her head.

"We'll let you know if we come up with something." She looked at the clock. "But now it's late. And I'd appreciate it if you, and your men, get out of my house."

Luke put his coffee mug down on the counter and nodded at Morgan.

"We'll get out of your house, but we'll still be watching. Those guys *will* make another attempt, probably not tonight but soon." He paused, his heart skipping a beat as he looked directly into her ice-blue eyes. "I know you know more than you're letting on and I understand why you don't want to open up to me. But I think you're just going to have to trust me on this one … your lives may depend on it."

Then he turned and walked off toward the front door.

* * *

MORGAN'S PULSE raced as she stared at Luke Hunter's retreating back. *Trust him?* She didn't think so.

He had a hell of a nerve showing up like this … after all these years and not one letter or phone call.

"We should listen to what he says," Celeste said quietly.

Morgan ground her teeth together. "And just *why* would we do that? He's a stranger to us now. I see no reason to trust him."

"But Morgan, Luke grew up here. You knew him better than any of us … don't you think he's telling the truth."

"*Knew* him … as in used to … I don't know him anymore. We have no idea where he's been for the past 10 years or what he's been up to. I wouldn't trust him any more than I'd trust a perfect stranger." Morgan felt her cheeks flush with anger.

"Well, he did bail us out tonight," Jolene offered. "Who knows what those men would have done if Luke and his guys weren't here."

Morgan shifted in her seat and looked across the hall into the living room. A chill crept up her spine thinking about the two men who broke in. What *were* they going to do? And what would have happened if Luke and his men weren't here?

"It's a mess in there," she said. "The china cabinet and everything in it is ruined. Nana's probably rolling over in her grave with all her good china smashed on the floor like that."

"No she's not," Celeste offered.

Everyone turned to stare at her.

Celeste shrugged. "Well, she's not. She doesn't care about that stuff anymore ... and she approves of Luke."

Morgan narrowed her eyes at Celeste. She wasn't sure what she thought about Celeste talking to their dead grandmother. She decided to change the subject.

"Did you guys have any luck deciphering the book?"

Celeste's face brightened. "We didn't get it all figured out, but we made good progress. The poetry book seems to be the key, but the journal ... well, there's just so much of it and it's mostly just a recording of the days events—weather, rough seas and so on."

"Oh, I was hoping there would be some sort of treasure clue." Jolene's face fell into a frown.

"I think that's too much to expect. All this talk of treasure and pirates is kind of silly. Most people don't have treasure buried in their yard," Morgan pointed out.

"Well, most people don't have an ancestor that sailed the seas in a ship either," Fiona said.

"Cal suggested we look at the book from a different angle. Try to find text that isn't in the format of the daily journal. There could be a clue." Celeste looked at Morgan. "Those men didn't break in here for nothing. I think you might have to admit there might be something to all this treasure stuff."

Morgan sighed. "Well I guess it won't hurt to look at the book some more. It's late and I'm tired. I'm heading off to bed and I suggest you all do the same."

Everyone murmured their agreement and the group headed for the main stair way together. Morgan's stomach clenched when they passed the living room. She turned to her sisters and Jake.

"I'm really glad none of us were badly hurt tonight."

"Me too," Fiona added then glanced at Morgan out of the corner of her eye. "But I agree with Luke. This isn't the end of our troubles with these treasure hunters. Maybe we should think about getting him on board with what we're doing?"

Morgan sighed. "Maybe. Let's see how it goes. I still don't see why we *need* him. And I wouldn't trust him as far as I could throw him."

"Yeah, we should think it over carefully," Celeste said as they made their way up the stairs. "And don't forget to trust your gut feeling, Morgan."

Morgan thought about that. Lately it had turned out to be smart— life saving even—to trust her gut feeling. But right now, her guts were all roiled up. The truth was she didn't know how she felt.

Seeing Luke again had caused a variety of emotions. She was mad, for sure, but she also couldn't help but notice how he seemed to have gotten even more handsome in the past ten years. She couldn't deny the way her stomach flip-flopped when she'd pulled off that mask or the way her senses had reveled in his familiar earthy clean smell.

She reached her bedroom door, said goodnight and tried to push all thoughts of Luke from her mind.

She didn't want … or need … him to help them and she'd be *damned* if she'd let him screw with her feelings again. The further away he stayed the better. She'd done just fine these past ten years without him and she sure as heck didn't need him now.

12

The next morning Morgan stumbled into the kitchen, heading straight for the coffee maker. She needed something stronger than her usual cup of herbal tea.

Fiona was already sitting at the island, sipping from a steaming mug, her red hair pulled back neatly in a ponytail at the nape of her neck.

"The strong stuff is in the left drawer." Fiona pointed to one of the kitchen drawers and Morgan grunted her thanks.

She put the K-cup in the coffee maker. The thirty seconds it took to produce the strong brew seemed like an eternity and she drummed her fingers on the counter hoping to speed it up. Finally, the mug was full and she took it over to the island.

Closing her eyes, she inhaled the pungent aroma then took a sip.

"Ahh … that's better," she said as the caffeine started to do its job.

"Well, it's not vanilla latte, but it does the trick," Fiona said. "Still, I want to stop at the coffee shop on the way to work and get my regular."

Morgan nodded. Fiona couldn't function without a latte of some sort in her bloodstream and she'd settled on vanilla as her favorite of late.

"Speaking of the shop, remind me to bring home some arnica and aloe vera to put on that cut Jolene got last night," Morgan said.

"I don't think you need to bother," Jolene said from the doorway.

Morgan's eye's widened when she saw Jolene's arm. She had unwrapped the bandage to reveal a long scar underneath—the wound had almost completely healed.

"But that's impossible," Morgan heard herself say as she and Fiona got up to inspect the wound.

"Well, it should be," Jolene said. "But apparently, it's not."

"How did that happen?" Morgan asked as Fiona pulled the carnelian stone from the middle of the gauze wrappings.

"Is that glowing?" Morgan squinted at the stone which appeared to be glowing bright orange from the inside. Fiona and Jolene bent closer.

"No, I think it's just the sunlight reflecting from the window." Jolene nodded toward the large kitchen window where the morning sun shone through.

Morgan ran her fingers across the scar. "This is amazing."

"There's a lot of strange things going on around us," Fiona added.

Morgan agreed—cuts that heal themselves, gut feelings that proved to be accurate, pirates, buried treasure, a cat that seemed to know what they were talking about and relatives that talked to Celeste from beyond the grave sure were strange.

"That's true." Celeste appeared in the doorway with Luke. "A lot of things that shouldn't be happening are. Maybe we should just accept it and go with the flow."

Morgan felt heat rise in her body at the sight of Luke. Anger … or something else?

"What are *you* doing here?" she demanded.

Luke pointed in the direction of the living room. "The window, remember?"

"Oh, right." Morgan looked toward the living room. "Hopefully that won't take long."

"About an hour. There's a real mess in there. Should we just pick everything up and toss it, or do you want to save it?"

Morgan's brow furrowed and she turned to ask her sisters, only to find they had snuck out of the room. "I don't know. Let me look."

They walked to the living room together, Morgan took care not to get too close to Luke—as if he had some disease she could catch.

Her heart clenched when she looked at the mess. The oak china cabinet lay on its front, the rounded glass doors shattered. She knew getting replacement glass would be expensive, but that was nothing compared to the antique china and crystal—family heirlooms that now lay in pieces on the floor. Those were priceless.

Battling the tears that stung the backs of her eyes, she squatted down and picked through the shards. There was nothing worth saving.

"I guess we should throw it out. The china cabinet we'll have repaired but everything else is broken." She ran her fingers through the pile, jerking her hand back when she felt the sharp sting of a shard of glass.

"Ouch!" She looked at her finger as it turned bright red.

Luke was next to her in an instant, grabbing her hand before she could react. "You cut yourself. Let me see."

Their eyes met and the past ten years melted away. Morgan's heart fluttered like a frightened bird. Then she remembered how hurt she'd been when Luke had chosen the military over her.

She wrenched her hand away.

"It's nothing," she said standing up and going back to the kitchen, feeling annoyed when she noticed Luke was following her.

She ran her finger under water then turned to face him. "Is there something else?"

"I was hoping you would have changed your mind about trusting me." Luke's green eyes stared into hers.

"And why would I do that?"

"We're both after the same thing. If we keep the lines of communication open it will be easier for both of us."

Morgan snorted. "Communication? I hope you're better at it now than you have been for the past ten years."

Luke ran his hands through his short cropped hair while Morgan wrapped her finger in a paper towel.

"Morgan, I'm sorry about all that. I couldn't stay

here and lead a cushy life while others were fighting for our country. I wanted to talk to you … to write, or call but I figured it was better for you if I didn't."

Morgan ripped her gaze from the pleading look in his eyes. She never could resist that look and he knew it. He was probably using it on purpose now to get her to tell him about the treasure.

"Well, I didn't need you to decide what was best for me then, and I certainly don't need you to do it now." She started toward the stairs, turning to look at him over her shoulder as she left the room. "I trust you can show yourself out."

Then, before the tears that were threatening could fall, she ran up to her room.

13

M organ breathed a sigh of relief when they pulled into the driveway after work. The day had been torturous. She was overtired and couldn't concentrate on anything. She'd had to toss out several herbal mixtures because she'd made them wrong. And the worst part was unwanted thoughts about Luke kept forming in her mind no matter how hard she tried to stop them.

When Celeste called to announce that she and Cal had found something in the journal, it was just the excuse Morgan and Fiona needed to close up early for the day.

As she walked up the porch steps into the house, Morgan felt a tingle in the back of her neck that was starting to become all too familiar. She whirled

around, but no one was there. *Was Luke watching her …
or the bad guys?*

Inside, Jolene, Cal and Celeste were huddled over
a piece of paper on the kitchen island.

"I hope you guys can help us decipher this poem
—it's a haiku," Celeste said.

Morgan and Fiona crossed over to the island and
Celeste slid the paper around so they could read it.

*Those seeking the map
Find joy in the turtle's dome
And under the rhomb*

MORGAN'S BROWS MASHED TOGETHER. "Huh? What's
this mean?"

"That's what we're trying to figure out," Jolene
said.

"Turtle? What turtle?" Fiona asked.

"And what the hell is a rhomb?" Morgan added.

"Who knows?" Jolene shrugged as she tapped something into her smart phone. "Oh, here, it says it's another
word for rhombus … you know, the geometric figure."

Morgan raised her brows. "This poem doesn't even make any sense. Could it be another code of some sort?"

"It could," Cal said. "Don't forget it was written long ago—and probably meant for someone who would understand the hidden meaning."

"The important thing is it seems to verify there is some sort of map." Celeste pointed to the first line of the poem.

"Or was," Morgan said.

"Right. Now if we only knew what it meant by turtle dome we might be on to something." Jolene settled back into her chair with a sigh.

Morgan felt something niggle at the back of her brain. Turtle. Dome. *Why did that seem familiar?*

Morgan snapped her fingers. "I've got it!"

She ran for the stairs to the attic with everyone following. At the top she surveyed the space, trying to remember where she had seen the little trunk.

"Mew."

She should have known Belladonna would be up here and she followed the sound.

"What is it?" Fiona's slightly out of breath voice came from behind her.

"I saw a domed box when I was up here before

and I think it was made of tortoise. That could be the *turtle's dome* mentioned in the poem."

The cat led them to an alcove and Morgan's heart clenched when she saw the box. She reached down and picked it up, holding it in front of her for the others to see.

Cal reached out and she handed it to him.

"This is really old," Cal said. "It definitely could be from the era of the poem."

His words sent a chill up Morgan's spine. *Could there really be a treasure map inside?*

"What are you waiting for? Open it up," Jolene said, leaning over Cal's shoulder to look at the box.

Cal held it out to Morgan. "Go ahead."

Morgan took the box in her hand, thinking how delicate it looked. A ripple of excitement surged through her like an electric current as she held the box. She grabbed the top and pulled.

Her heart sunk like a stone.

"It won't open." She tried to pull harder, but the box was sealed tight.

"It's probably locked." Cal pointed to the tiny keyhole on the front.

Morgan's excitement deflated. "What are the odds of finding the key in this?" She spread her hands to indicate the vast space.

"Let me see." Jolene held out her hand and Morgan placed the box in it.

Jolene squinted at the lock, turned the box this way and that then rummaged in an open trunk that was sitting on the floor. She pulled out an antique hairpin which was about eight inches long and had a large pearl on the end. She stuck the pin end into the keyhole, wiggled it around and the box popped open.

Morgan's heart dropped when she looked inside. It was empty.

"Hey, where'd you learn to do that?" Fiona furrowed her brow at Jolene.

"Oh, I've been looking into some private investigator stuff online … just a little trick I picked up." Jolene shrugged.

"Figures, it's empty," Morgan said. "I guess it was silly to think an old treasure map would still be in here after all these years."

"It's a nice box though." Celeste took the box from Jolene.

"Very nice … and very valuable," Cal said.

Morgan shrugged. "I guess we should put it back."

"Wait," Cal said. "A lot of times, these old boxes had false bottoms."

Morgan peered over Celeste's shoulder into the box.

"It doesn't look like it has a false bottom," she said, bending down to look at the box from underneath.

She held out her hand and Celeste put the box in it. The inside bottom was an indigo blue velvety material—worn and faded over the years. She could barely make out the pattern, oddly shaped diamonds in gold.

A jolt of electricity shot through her heart as she remembered the last line of the poem "*and under the rhomb*". She jerked her head in Jolene's direction. "What shape is a rhombus?"

Jolene made a face. "I think it's like a diamond with equal sides or something. Why?"

Morgan didn't answer. She was too busy ripping out the velvet lining. Her stomach flip-flopped when she saw the aged parchment underneath. Gently, she reached into the box and pulled it out.

Celeste, Fiona and Jolene gasped as she held it up by the corner.

"It's the map!"

"Careful, that looks awfully brittle," Cal said. "Let's bring it over to this bureau.

He indicated a large Eastlake style bureau a few

feet away and Morgan carried it over and spread it out on the marble top.

The dry parchment was tattered on the edges, the ink faded, but there was enough for them to make out a small map and some writing. The map depicted a point of land with water on three sides. Arrows pointed toward a large tree and the writing gave further directions.

"That looks like our land." Fiona looked out the window.

"Yes!" Jolene pointed excitedly. "Here's the Atlantic on this side and the channel leading to the cove on the other ... there's no big tree there though."

"Maybe there was a tree three hundred years ago," Celeste offered.

"We need to copy this so that we don't damage the original," Cal said.

"Right," Morgan agreed, looking around for a paper and pencil.

"There's a paper and pencil over by the bookcase, where I copied some of the journal," Celeste said and Cal started off in that direction.

"Do you really think this is our yard?" Fiona asked.

"Sure looks like it." Jolene's eyes sparkled as she studied the map.

"There could be buried treasure right out there." Celeste pointed out the window.

Morgan looked out to where Celeste was pointing, a familiar tingle forming in her lower belly. Even though her logical brain kept telling her the thought of pirate treasure being buried in her yard was ridiculous, her gut instincts were telling her something big was about to happen.

14

The sun was about to set by the time Celeste had copied the map. They stood in the side yard, huddled around the copy, shovels at the ready. The wind from the ocean licked at the edges of the paper, threatening to tear it from Cal's hand.

"It says start at the tree. Anyone know where the tree was?" Cal asked.

Morgan didn't remember any tree, so she tried to figure it out by looking at the map.

"Meow." Belladonna sat off to the left, her tail twitching in the grass.

"From looking at the map, it looks like the tree was right about where Belladonna is." Morgan was getting used to the cat showing up in the exact right spot and at the right time.

"Okay, it looks like it says thirty paces east." Cal

walked over to Belladonna's spot, then turned east and took thirty steps. Everyone ran over to stand beside him.

"Then ten steps toward the point. What's that mean?" Celeste asked.

"I assume the point of the cliff." Cal took the ten steps.

"Now three quarter turn as the sun rises."

"Does that mean toward the east? That's where the sun rises," Jolene said.

"I guess so. Let's try that." Morgan watched Cal turn then take a few more steps indicated by the directions on the map. After a few more turns and paces he stopped.

"Well, if I followed the directions correctly, this is the spot." Cal pointed to an area of grass right in front of him.

The five of them looked at each other uncertainly.

Should they start digging?

Jolene broke the ice by plunging her shovel into the grass and the rest followed suit.

Morgan jabbed her shovel into the rocky ground. It wasn't as easy as she thought it was going to be and she had to jump on the edge of the blade in order to get it to sink in. She removed a small shovel full of dirt and placed it aside.

"How deep do you think this thing is buried?"

Cal shrugged. "Who knows? Probably not too deep, I mean it's not like whoever buried it in 1722 had machinery. They would have had to dig by hand. Just like we are."

Morgan wiped a bead of sweat from her forehead with the back of her hand. "Well I hope he went easy with the digging, this could take a long time."

"That's why I called in a favor from a friend," Jolene said as her cellphone chimed. She looked at the display, then jogged toward the front of the house.

Morgan raised an eyebrow at Fiona who shrugged and continued digging. Morgan's enthusiasm waned as she looked in the hole.

"I don't see any sign of treasure," she said.

"We're not that far down ye—"

Fiona's words were cut off by the sound of an engine coming from the side of the house and Morgan turned to see Jolene directing a small Bobcat bulldozer toward them. She gladly set her shovel aside and waved them over.

"This is the favor you called in?"

"Yep," Jolene said. "It pays to have friends that

owe you. This is Randy." Jolene went through the round of introductions between her sisters, Cal and the Bobcat operator.

They stood back while Randy operated the machine, expertly digging just a little bit at a time so as not to damage whatever might be in there.

Out of the corner of her eye, Morgan could see Belladonna about fifteen feet away, watching them, her tail flicking animatedly. She tried to focus on the digging, but her attention was drawn more and more toward the cat who was now digging furiously.

Morgan walked over and squatted next to her. "What are you doing Belladonna?"

"Meow!" The cat glanced over at her, then resumed her frenzied digging.

Morgan reached out to pet her, but the cat moved away, looked at her reproachfully, and attacked the hole from another angle.

Morgan noticed she'd dug about six inches down. Peering into the hole, her heart lurched when she saw a sliver of light reflecting off something.

What was that?

She reached into the hole and Belladonna sat back on her haunches, proceeding to clean the dirt from her front paws. Morgan's fingers closed on something cool and smooth, about the size of a quarter. She pulled it out.

Adrenalin shot through her body as she held it up to the light. The fading sun glinted off the small round object like it was gold. Morgan's heartbeat quickened when she realized it probably *was* gold.

But what was it?

She laid it flat in her palm to take a better look. It looked like it could be some sort of coin, but the edges were unevenly cut. There was writing and images on it, but they were well worn. One side had what looked like a cross in the middle, the other a grid which reminded her of tic tac toe.

"Hey guys …" She rose to her feet holding the coin out for them to see.

Cal's eyes grew wide. He came over and held his hand out for the coin.

"Where did you get this?"

"In the hole Belladonna was digging." Morgan gestured toward the hole and Cal looked down at it, then back at the coin.

"This is an 8 Escudo—a gold Spanish coin. It dates to the early 1700s. This thing is worth about ten grand."

Morgan looked at the Bobcat, then down at the little hole that had produced the coin.

"Do you think we could be digging in the wrong spot?"

"I don't know … we're digging where the map said." Cal rubbed his chin. "Unless the map was in some sort of code, like instead of going right we should have gone left."

He whistled toward the other group and they stopped and turned to look at him.

"Hey, bring that thing over here. Morgan found something." He held up the coin and everyone came over to admire it.

"I found it in this hole. We should dig it out, just in case there is more."

"What made you decide to dig over here?" Fiona asked.

"I didn't. It was Belladonna." Morgan nodded toward the cat who was now laying on the top granite step at the kitchen door.

Fiona raised an eyebrow and Belladonna stared at them, flicking her tail.

The Bobcat started up and Cal directed the operator to dig slowly, only a little bit at a time.

Morgan and her sisters stared anxiously into the hole, waiting. For what, she had no idea, but she had a feeling she'd know it when she saw it.

It didn't take long. She heard a metallic scrape

and saw something silver flash in the hole. Cal must have heard it too because he held up his hand.

"Hold up!"

The Bobcat shovel stopped in midair. Cal bent down and reached into the hole, lifting out a silver box. It was beautiful with a flowery carved, repousse design and gold details on the corners. Beautiful, but small, Morgan thought. Cal passed it around, handing it to Celeste, who admired it for a minute then handed it to Jolene.

How much treasure could that thing possibly hold?

She was about to reach for the box when a voice cut through the air behind her and stopped her cold.

"Hold it right there!"

15

Morgan's heart froze as she turned toward the sound of the voice—Sheriff Overton.

He ambled over to them, the ever present toothpick sticking out of the side of his mouth, a satisfied smirk plastered on his face.

"Do you have a permit to dig here?" He gestured toward the two holes.

"Permit? Why would we need that? It's our property." Morgan stood with her hands on her hips. She could see Jolene with the box sneaking away, off to the side behind Overton and tried her best to draw his attention away from her.

"Town ordinance. A permit is required for all machined digging." He nodded toward the Bobcat.

Morgan flicked her eyes toward Fiona who

shrugged. *Was he telling the truth?* Morgan wished she'd paid more attention to the town laws.

Overton walked over to the hole and looked in. "What are you digging for? Or are you digging a hole to hide your next dead body?"

Morgan's shoulders stiffened and she fought the desire to slap the smirk off his face.

"We're testing out soil conditions for a special herb garden," Morgan lied, sending a warning glance to the others.

Overton furrowed his brow. "Is that so?"

Morgan nodded. "Yep, we're going to plant some herbs that need deep, sandy soil, so we were digging around to find the best spot."

"Yeah, you know how hard it is to grow plants without the right conditions," Fiona added amidst nods from everyone else.

Overton walked over to the other hole and peered in, then turned and narrowed his eyes at Morgan. He took a pad of paper out of his pocket.

"I'll have to write you up. That's a five hundred dollar fine." Overton smiled.

Morgan's heart plummeted. They barely had enough to pay the taxes on the house and now this?

"But we're only digging a couple of little holes. We're filling them in right away," she protested.

"Don't matter." He wiggled the toothpick back and forth as he wrote.

Morgan's cheeks grew warm with anger but she held herself back from doing something she might regret later. At least Overton hadn't seen the coin or the box. Her gut feeling told her it was better to just take the ticket and get him out of there as soon as possible then to instigate something that might cause him to linger.

"This needs to be paid in ten days or I might have to exercise my right to put out a warrant on you." Overton stared at Morgan as he ripped the paper from the pad. "And put you in jail ... where you belong."

Morgan stared Overton down as she took the paper. "Is that all?"

"I think I have cause to look around some."

Morgan's stomach lurched as he started over by the house. She knew he was looking for any little thing he could find to use as an excuse to get some sort of warrant to look inside.

"Sheriff! Dispatch just called in, there's an accident over on Route 1," one of the uniformed cops yelled from the side of the house.

Overton grunted then spun around and ambled off, turning only long enough to shoot Morgan a warning glance.

"Don't forget to pay that promptly."

Morgan's shoulders relaxed as he rounded the side of the house.

"What was that all about? I've never had that happen before," Randy asked.

"Don't ask," Morgan said. "Overton doesn't like us and he'll use any excuse to hassle us."

The boy shrugged. "It's getting pretty dark—I assume you guys are done with the Bobcat, right?"

"Yes, we got what we were looking for. Thanks so much for helping us."

"Umm … You won't say anything about what we dug up, will you?" Celeste added.

"Mum's the word. Jolene already swore me to secrecy." He gave a "scouts honor" sign, started up the Bobcat and headed toward the front.

"Speaking of Jolene, where did she run off to with that box?" Fiona asked.

"I don't know. But I have a feeling it's a good thing Overton didn't see that fancy box or the coin. The less he knows about what's going on here, the better."

* * *

CAL GRABBED A SHOVEL. "I'll fill these holes back in, you guys go inside."

Fiona and Celeste headed toward the kitchen door on the side, but Morgan went toward the front —she wanted to make sure Overton was really gone. Her mind started to wander to the box they had pulled from the hole.

What was in it?

She couldn't help but think it seemed pretty small to contain much of a treasure. She glanced back. *Maybe there was more buried deeper in the hole?*

She hesitated between going forward to the front or back to look deeper into the hole. The front door won. She wanted to see what was in the box and they could always dig it out more, later. She stepped forward before looking where she was going and ran smack into—

Luke Hunter.

"What the—"

"Whoa. You should watch where you're going."

Luke smiled at her causing her heart to skitter around in her ribcage. He had put his arm on her waist to keep her from toppling over and she noticed he hadn't bothered to remove it. It felt familiar, exciting and annoying all at the same time.

"You scared the crap out of me. You shouldn't sneak up on people like that." She took a step backward and Luke dropped his hand to his side.

"Sorry. I saw the ruckus and wanted to know what was going on." Luke thrust his chin toward the holes.

Morgan bit her bottom lip.

Should she tell him?

She didn't want to. Probably because she was still hurt about the way he left ten years ago. She felt like he'd betrayed her then and didn't see what would stop him from doing it now. Then again, he *had* saved them the other night and he was too smart to accept the lame gardening excuse she'd given to Overton.

"We found a map in the attic. A treasure map," she said.

Luke raised his eyebrows. "And did you find a treasure in one of those holes?"

Morgan shrugged. "Not really. We found a coin and a small box."

Luke cursed under his breath making Morgan's stomach clench.

"What?" She narrowed her eyes, was he mad they found something or mad that it was so small?

"I'm sure those treasure hunters are watching you

from somewhere." Luke glanced out into the Atlantic Ocean. "They probably saw that you dug something up and now they will be coming after you for it."

"Well, they already broke into our house once. I figured they'd be coming back." Morgan looked out at the wooded area, then past it to the ocean. *Was there a boat out there beyond her scope of vision with high powered binoculars trained on her house?*

Luke grabbed her upper arms, forcing her to look back at him. She noticed his green eyes were hard and cold.

"Morgan, this is serious. These guys are killers." She saw his eyes soften. He reached out and brushed a lock of hair away from her forehead, causing a riot of emotions to run through her.

"I couldn't stand it if anything happened to you —you have to come clean with me and tell me everything you know. *And* let me know what you plan to do next."

She let out a sigh. "I don't know what was in the box and I'm not sure what we'll do next. I guess it depends on what's in the box."

"And what about Overton, what did he want?"

"To hassle us, as usual. I told you before how he has it in for us … and I have no idea why."

"Yeah, I don't trust him. What about this Jake guy that was with Fiona? Can you trust him or is he in close with Overton?"

Morgan thought back to how Jake had risked his own job and gone against Overton to help prove she was innocent in the Littlefield murder. She'd trust him with her life.

"Jake is totally trustworthy. He doesn't like Overton either. In fact, Overton is doing everything he can to keep Jake away from the case of the dead guy on the cliff."

Luke nodded. "Okay. Good. We need all the people on our side we can get."

Morgan shuffled her feet. She felt awkward and unsure of herself. Part of her wanted to bolt into the house and the other part of her wanted to stand here with Luke all night.

She gave herself a mental head slap. *What was she thinking?*

"We cleaned up the mess in your living room and we're getting the glass replaced in the china cabinet. Sorry about your grandma's china, I remember how much you loved it."

Morgan's heart softened another notch toward him. *He remembered how much she loved that china.*

A variety of words tried to battle their way from her brain to her mouth, but she only managed to get one out. "Thanks."

"Okay, well if you find out anything else, or see anyone or anything suspicious call me right away." He reached into his pocket and pulled out a black business card with nothing but a phone number on it in silver. Morgan turned the card over, the back was blank.

"That's my private cell number. Call me no matter what time of day or night."

Morgan's stomach did a somersault as he turned to go and she stared at his back, unable to move. After a few steps he turned to face her again.

"In the meantime, my men and I will be keeping a close eye on you … and your sisters."

Then he turned and trotted off toward the woods.

* * *

SHE ALMOST CALLED AFTER HIM.

Then she remembered that she had no idea where he'd been or what he'd been doing for the past ten years. For all she knew, he was the head of these treasure hunting pirates and was just trying to worm the information out of her.

Still, for a few minutes, it had seemed like old times. Like the Luke she'd once loved. She'd have to be careful. She couldn't let herself get hurt by him again.

Stuffing his business card in her back pocket, she ran up the porch steps into the house, pausing only for a second to glance over in the direction that Luke had disappeared in.

Was he watching her now?

The thought made her feel safe … and a little creeped out at the same time.

She turned back and opened the front door, heading in the direction of the kitchen where she could hear everyone talking.

"Can you guys believe this? What a jerk." She slapped the citation Overton had given her on the counter.

"I know. He really hates you guys," Cal said.

"Good thing we dug up this coin, looks like we're going to need some extra money." Celeste held up the escudo and turned to Cal. "Are you sure this is real?"

"Of course. I *am* an expert you know." He raised his eyebrows at Celeste.

Celeste laughed. "I know, sorry."

"I can lend you guys some money if you need it to pay that right away. I'm sure I can find a buyer for the coin." He pointed at the citation.

Morgan looked at her sisters. "Should we sell the coin? I'm not sure what to do but I know the money would sure come in handy."

"Fine by me. Hopefully there will be plenty more inside this box." Jolene held up the little box they had taken from the hole and shook it carefully.

"I don't hear anything rattling around inside." Morgan's brow creased as she looked at the box. "Did you open it?"

"We were waiting for you." Fiona looked at Morgan out of the corner of her eye. "What were you doing out there with Luke?"

Morgan felt her cheeks grow warm. "What? He wanted to know what was going on. That's all."

"Oh?"

Morgan turned to the cupboard on the pretense of getting a coffee mug.

"He saw us digging and was wondering what we were up to. Anyone want tea?"

"What did you tell him?" Celeste asked.

Morgan shrugged as she rummaged for a tea bag.

"I kind of had to tell him we dug up the box there, but I didn't tell him much else."

"Why not? He bailed us out last night." Celeste tapped her finger on her lips. "Come to think of it, that was probably him that chased off those muggers."

"What muggers?" Cal wrinkled his brows at Celeste.

"Yeah, what muggers?" Fiona and Jolene said at the same time.

"Oops." Celeste shrugged. "Well, there's really no sense in keeping it from everyone. I think we all know that we're in danger here with the break in last night and all."

"I guess you're right," Morgan said. "Celeste and I got jumped the other day when we went to see Cal."

"What? Why didn't you say something?" Cal's eyes clouded over with concern.

"Well, we got away. Celeste kicked the crap out of the guys and we ran off. Then some other guys came out of nowhere and I guess they took care of the attackers."

"Hey I wonder if those other guys were Luke's guys?" Celeste said.

Morgan remembered how she had thought she'd seen Luke that day. "I think it might have been, now that I remember, I thought one of them looked like Luke."

"And you still don't trust him?" Fiona raised an eyebrow at her.

"You don't trust Luke?" Cal turned to Morgan.

"Well, it's not that I don't trust him. It's just that we don't know anything about him anymore."

Cal shrugged. "Jeez, Morgan. We've known Luke since we were kids and he was always a good guy. A few years in the military probably hasn't changed that. Are you sure you aren't letting your emotions get in the way of your better judgment?"

Morgan bristled. "I just think we need to be really careful."

"I know you're still hurt about the way he left, but I think he was doing what he thought was best for you," Cal said.

"Yeah, he seems like he really *is* on our side," Fiona added.

"Well, we'll see. I know we can trust each other and anything else … well." Morgan shrugged, looking at the little box that Jolene had set on the breakfast bar island in front of her.

"Forget about Luke. Let's open this thing up and see what's inside.

* * *

Jolene pushed the box toward Morgan. "Go ahead."

Morgan stared at it. It wasn't very big, not much bigger than a couple of decks of cards.

"It doesn't look like it could hold much of a treasure." Fiona sounded disappointed.

"You can say that again. I was wondering if there might be more in the holes," Morgan said. "I mean a tiny box like this hardly seems worth all the trouble we've had with these pirate guys and everything."

"Are you going to open it and find out, or what?" Jolene's fingers drummed on the counter.

Morgan looked at the front. This one didn't have a lock like the last one, it had a button. Morgan pressed it and the lid flew open. Her stomach dropped—the box was empty except for a brittle piece of paper.

Fiona, Jolene, Cal and Celeste bent their heads over the box to look inside.

"That's it?" Jolene scrunched up her face.

"Maybe this one has a false bottom too?" Fiona crouched down so that the bottom of the box was eye level.

Morgan carefully picked out the piece of paper

and laid it on the island in front of her. The faded swirly writing was similar to that in the journal.

You'll find the key you seek beneath the tree we vowed our love.

"Oh geez, another cryptic clue. What the heck does that mean?" Jolene blew out a breath strong enough to cause her wavy bangs to puff out.

"I don't know. What tree do you think it means?" Fiona asked.

"Who knows? That tree could be long gone by now—the note was written almost three hundred years ago," Morgan pointed out.

Fiona picked up the box, inspecting it from all angles. "I don't think there's any hidden compartment in this one. Geez, what a letdown."

"Yeah, I knew all this pirate stuff was silly," Morgan added.

"Well, I guess it gives us something to think about," Cal said. "In the meantime, I'm going to setup camp in the spare bedroom."

"What?" Morgan scrunched her eyebrows at him.

"Are you being stalked by one of your girlfriends and need to hide out here?"

Everyone giggled. Cal was known for being a ladies man but he often had a couple of girls going at the same time which sometimes got dangerous for him.

"No, Miss smarty pants. I'm staying here until you guys are out of danger. I don't want to leave you guys alone to get attacked again."

"And Jake is staying too. In fact, he should be here any minute," Fiona added.

Morgan pursed her lips. Normally she would argue. As the oldest Blackmoore, she felt like she could take care of her sisters by herself, but her common sense prevailed. They'd already been attacked and broken into. Having two strong guys here couldn't hurt.

"Okay. Thanks." She smiled at Cal.

"Come on, I'll help you pick out a room." Celeste stood up. The house had twelve bedrooms. Some were closed off, but they still had quite a few guest rooms for Cal to choose from.

Morgan suppressed a yawn. "Yeah, I'm pretty tired. I think I'll go upstairs and read or something. Maybe I'll get an inspiration about what "*the tree we vowed our love*" means."

"Let's hope so," Fiona said. "I don't want to be looking over my shoulder for pirates for much longer."

Morgan nodded. "Or worrying about finding dead guys on the cliff."

16

Morgan was surprised that she'd slept so well the night before. She hated to admit it, but knowing that Cal and Jake were in the house and Luke had an army of men watching them made her feel secure.

Too bad she hadn't come up with any ideas about what the writing on the paper meant.

"I think today is going to be a good day," Fiona said as she opened the door to *Sticks and Stones*.

"Well, no one tried to break in and no dead bodies appeared on the cliff, so it's already shaping up to be pretty good in my eyes," Morgan replied as she turned the sign on the door to "Open".

"I have something for you." Fiona rummaged in her jewelry case, coming up with a pendant on a chain. The stone was a rich honey brown, shaded from dark to light.

Morgan held her hand out and the gemstone sparked as one sister handed it to another.

"It's tiger's eye." Fiona said. "It will help protect you."

Morgan narrowed her eyes at the stone. A week ago she might have scoffed at the idea of a rock protecting her against anything, but after seeing Jolene's wound heal so quickly and the odd things that had been happening, she didn't know what to think anymore. She fastened the necklace around her neck as she looked out the back window of the shop.

"Hopefully I won't need to be protected."

Fiona shrugged. "Better safe, than sorry."

Morgan pursed her lips as she looked into the forest behind the shop. The birds hopped between branches, squirrels scurried around on the ground. Out of the corner of her eye she saw something white streak by.

Was that who she thought it was?

She opened the window and poked her head out.

"What are you doing?" Fiona asked.

"You won't believe who I thought I just saw."

"In the woods? Who would be there? Oh wait … you don't mean?"

"Yep, it's her."

Morgan stared at Belladonna who sat at the bottom of the ancient oak tree, staring back at her. This wasn't the first time the cat had shown up here and Morgan had no idea how she even knew the way. Granted, it was only about a mile from their house, but Morgan's stomach clenched at the thought of the cat running around in traffic.

Fiona came to the window. "I don't know what gets into her."

"Who knows?" Morgan shrugged. "I guess we should bring her inside. At least we can make sure she gets a ride home with us and isn't out wandering the streets."

Morgan went out through the back door of the cottage. Belladonna had started digging under the tree and scooted away from Morgan when she tried to pick her up.

"Belladonna, come."

The cat ignored her.

"Want a treat?"

Belladonna dug even faster.

"You know cats don't fall for that stuff." Fiona said. "What is she digging for?"

"I have no idea. Probably a mouse or something."

"Mew!" The cat glanced back at them then returned to digging.

"Well, it's an old tree ..."

Morgan didn't hear the rest of the sentence. She was busy looking up at the initials carved in the tree. Her heart jerked as if someone had zapped it with electricity.

You'll find the key you seek beneath the tree we vowed our love.

"This is it!" Morgan's mind whirled. *Did they have any shovels here?*

"Huh?" Fiona frowned at her.

"This is the tree from the clue in the box. Look at the initials." She pointed upwards and Fiona bent her head back.

"IB and MB. Do you think that's Isaiah Blackmoore?"

Morgan nodded. "Yep. This land has been in our family for generations. In fact, I think we owned all of it around here at one time." Morgan grabbed a hoe and trowel they used for putting flowers in the front garden from the side of the cottage.

"Here you use the hoe to loosen stuff up. I'll dig with the trowel." Morgan handed the hoe to Fiona.

Belladonna sat back and watched the sister's dig. They fell into a rhythm, Fiona churning up the dirt and Morgan digging around after her.

Morgan was just starting to wonder if they should close the shop when her trowel scraped against metal.

"I've got something!"

She reached into the hole, her stomach flipping as her fingers slid over cold metal. She brushed away the dirt to reveal gleaming silver.

"What is it?" Fiona had squatted beside her.

"I think it's a box." Morgan wiggled the corner and it slid out of the dirt.

She held it up, feeling slightly disappointed. The box was small—smaller than the last one. It fit in the palm of her hand and was only about an inch high. The finish looked like a match to the last box, finely detailed silver in a flower pattern.

"That's kind of small. What's in it?" Fiona asked.

Morgan looked at the front. It had a push clasp, similar to the other box. She felt a stab of disappointment. The box was too small for any real treasure.

She pressed the clasp and the box popped open as if the hinges were just oiled yesterday. Morgan stared at the contents.

An old skeleton key sat gleaming on a blue velvet lining.

"A key?" Fiona asked.

"I wonder what it goes to?"

"I hope it's something good, this treasure hunt is getting tedious."

Morgan nodded. Maybe her ancestor had a warped sense of humor and all these clues led to nothing … or maybe the treasure had been taken years ago. But if it was, why would the treasure hunters be so keen to find it? They must have something pretty solid to think the treasure was still around.

Morgan felt the hairs on the back her neck stand up, her heart lurched. In her excitement of figuring out the clue, she'd forgotten that the treasure hunters could be watching.

"We better get inside," she said glancing around. "They could be watching us and we don't want them to know we dug up another clue."

"Right," Fiona said as they quickly shoved the dirt back into place, then scurried in the back door, leaving the trowel and hoe leaning against the cottage. Belladonna squeaked through in between their feet and found a sunny spot to curl up and sleep in.

The girls stood in the center of the shop looking at the shiny key that lay flat in the palm of Morgan's hand.

"I wonder what it goes to?" Morgan asked.

"I hope it's something good, this treasure hunt is getting tedious."

"The logical place to look would be—"

Morgan was interrupted by the sound of the door being jerked open. The girls swiveled their heads toward the door and Morgan's stomach dropped when she saw a giant of a man standing inside the door way.

"I'll take that," The giant said as he turned the shop sign to "Closed" and slammed the door shut.

Morgan closed her hand and took a step backwards as the man lunged for the key. Her heart pounded as he advanced on them, backing the girls further into the shop.

"Hand it over and I won't have to hurt 'ya." His harsh, angry voice sent chills up Morgan's spine.

"No," she said.

His eyebrows shot up and his face turned red, then he lurched forward grabbing for her arm.

Some of Celeste's quick moves must have worn off on her because Morgan shot her elbow out at the exact right moment and it connected with his nose making a sickening crunching sound.

Blood spurted out of the giant's nose and his hands flew up to cover it. He bent forward at the waist, stumbled and stepped on Belladonna's tail.

Belladonna screeched and flew through the air, landing on his back with her claws fully extended.

He let out a wail, flailing with one hand toward his back as he straightened up. Morgan saw Belladonna slide down his back, leaving a trail of claw marks. He spun around, reaching for the cat.

"Damn cat!"

Belladonna flew up to the top of the bookcase and sat there hissing and spitting at him. Out of the corner of her eye, Morgan could see Fiona grappling behind her, her hands flailing around the display where she kept her geodes. Her right hand found the largest one which was about twice the size of a candlepin bowling ball.

The giant turned his attention back toward the girls. His face was twisted in anger as he closed the distance between them quicker than seemed humanly possible.

His arm shot out toward Morgan. Her heart lurched in her chest as his large hand wrapped around her throat and squeezed. She tried to struggle, but that only made it worse, her vision started to fade. Pin pricks of stars floated in front of her eyes as she watched Fiona smash the geode right into the giant's face.

He went down with a crash and lay still on the floor.

Morgan sucked in a deep breath.

"Are you okay?" Fiona stared at her.

"Yeah." Her voice sounded raspy and her fingers flew to her throat which felt raw.

"We better tie him up in case he wakes up before I can call Luke," Morgan said, thankful she had put Luke's card in her pocket this morning before work.

Fiona ripped open a drawer and pulled out some twine. "I hope he's not dead." She looked at him uncertainly.

Morgan bent over the still body. Belladonna hopped onto his stomach and sat there.

"He's breathing. He's not dead." Morgan held her hand out for the twine. She had no idea how to tie someone up to restrain them but she'd have to do her best.

"Help me flip him over, then we can tie his arms behind him."

The girls got on one side and pried him over on to his back. Morgan caught a glimpse of Fiona's wrist as they pushed him over and her heartbeat quickened. The stones on Fiona's bracelet were glowing.

"Look at your bracelet!"

Fiona looked down. "What the heck? It's never done that before."

The girls were staring down at the bracelet when the door to their shop jerked open a second time.

17

Morgan'ss heart jolted and she ripped her gaze away from the bracelet, bracing herself for another fight.

"Luke!"

"What happened? Are you okay?"

Luke was at her side in a second, his green eyes clouded with concern.

"I'm fine," she said, her voice still a little raspy. Then she motioned toward the giant on the floor. 'This guy must be one of those treasure hunters."

"Your throat—it's all red. Did he hurt you?" Luke put his hand tenderly on her neck to inspect it. Morgan's pulse quickened, a warm glow spreading throughout her body.

Her hand flew up to her throat on instinct. "He tried to strangle me, but I'm okay."

Luke stared at her for a few seconds more, and then narrowed his eyes at the guy on the floor.

"What did he want?"

Morgan caught Fiona's glance and knew her sister was right. It was time to tell Luke everything.

"Remember the box we dug up yesterday?" Morgan asked as Luke opened the door, making hand motions apparently to someone outside.

"Yes." He glanced at her while he held the door open for three guys who got busy tying up the giant.

"It only had a piece of paper in it, but that paper was a clue," Fiona added.

"A clue that led us to the giant tree out back. We dug around and found this." Morgan opened her fist to show him the key.

"What does it go to?" Luke asked.

"We don't know." Morgan flipped the key over. "We've been going on some sort of treasure hunt. First we found a passage in this old journal we had in the attic. That led us to an old box that had a map in it. We followed the map and dug the holes yesterday, which had another box where the clue was to dig under the tree here."

Luke raised his eyebrows at her. "And the dead pirate in your yard. What do you know about him?"

"Nothing," Morgan said. "Well, except that

Overton said he was found with a manifest from a ship called the *Ocean's Revenge* that was supposedly captained by some relative of ours. That's why we went to look in the journal in the attic in the first place."

Luke nodded. "Is there anything else I should know?"

Morgan shook her head.

"Well, there is one thing … maybe two," Fiona interjected. "Morgan and Celeste were attacked the other day."

"Yeah, I saw that. Celeste has a mean karate kick."

"So, you *were* there," Morgan said.

"Yep, we've been here watching things for a while." Luke stepped aside to let the men drag the giant outside. "What was the other thing?"

"Oh, I think Fiona is talking about the boats, right?" Morgan cocked an eyebrow at her sister.

"Yep. A customer said she saw boats going back and forth in the water around the entrance to the cove at two in the morning," Fiona explained.

Luke frowned. "Have you seen the boats? How many nights did they do this?"

"We haven't seen them." Morgan looked at Fiona. "I think it was only one night, right?"

Fiona nodded. "As far as I know."

Luke rubbed his chin. "They were probably trolling for sunken treasure."

"That's what Jake said!"

Luke nodded. "Sometimes pirates would sink their ships on purpose in an out of the way place so no one else would get the treasure. They would come back and retrieve it later. The treasure hunters were looking for a sunken ship ... but if they haven't come back that probably means they didn't find any evidence of one."

"So then why are they still bugging us?" Fiona asked.

"They didn't find any evidence *in the water*. But they sure do think there is something in this area, so now they are going to focus on the land."

Morgan shuddered. "So we just have to find it first then, right?"

"It's not really that simple. And you guys shouldn't be digging around without talking to me. In addition to sinking their ships, pirates were well known for booby-trapping the places they buried their treasure—to protect it from thieves. Whoever came digging around to steal it would meet with an untimely and unpleasant end. You guys need to be careful that you don't get caught in a booby trap when you are digging."

Morgan's eyes went wide and she ventured a look out to the tree in back.

Luke read her mind. "That's right, you could have been hurt … or killed … today or last night. The treasure hunters aren't your only worry here."

Luke paused and his green eyes turned serious as he looked at Fiona, then back at Morgan.

"Now that they know you are getting closer to the treasure, they'll probably step up their efforts. We've reduced their numbers, but I think there are still a few of them out there and they'll stop at nothing. I know you guys like to take care of yourselves but I'd like to have some of my guys in the house with you," Luke said.

"We have Cal and Jake staying over." Morgan stuck out her chin, stubbornly.

Luke nodded. "So far nothing too bad has happened —we diffused the situation with the break in and you and Celeste were able to outwit the attackers the other day. But you might not always be so lucky." He narrowed his eyes at Morgan. "By the way, how did you know to pull Celeste back from that alley just at the right moment?"

Morgan felt her stomach clench. *Should she tell him*

the truth about the strange things that were happening? Her gut instincts told her "yes".

"I just had a gut feeling, and Celeste said that Nana told her to tell me to trust my gut feelings. It worked out pretty good in that case."

"Your Nana? Isn't she dead?" Luke switched his gaze from Morgan to Fiona.

"Yes," Fiona said. "Apparently Celeste has been talking to dead people. You know how she was always kind of spiritual what with all her meditation and stuff. I guess she connected with '*the other side*'."

Luke looked down at Morgan and shook his head. "Carnelian stones that heal wounds, dead people giving you guys advice, and gut feelings that save you from getting abducted … I guess it's going to be a challenge for me to get reacquainted with the Black-moore girls."

Luke took Morgan's hand and her heart fluttered as he pulled her to him. "I have some things to take care of, but I'm coming to your house tonight. By the way things are heating up, I think I need to keep you girls under very close surveillance. And I'm not taking no for an answer."

Then he kissed her cheek, turned on his heel and left.

Morgan's heart took off like a thoroughbred at

the starting gate. She felt that familiar pull in her lower belly. She had to admit, the thought of Luke keeping them under close surveillance wasn't really all that unpleasant.

But then she felt a warning tingle in her gut. After all the hurt he had caused her ten years ago, she couldn't let herself fall for Luke Hunter all over again. Could she?

18

"We need to get home and into the attic to look for the box that key opens." Fiona picked up the geode that still lay on the floor and returned it to its place on the shelf.

"Right." Morgan stood staring at the door Luke had just disappeared through, wondering what his kiss on the cheek meant. It was really just a peck. But was it a friendly peck or something more?

"Earth to Morgan." Fiona was standing at the door, Belladonna under one arm.

"Oh, sorry." Morgan followed her out the door and the three of them climbed into Fiona's old truck.

"We should call Celeste and Jolene and tell them what we found ... and about the attack," Fiona said as she pulled out onto the main road.

Morgan pulled out her cell phone and made the calls.

"They're both home and so is Cal. Looks like we'll have plenty of help." Belladonna had curled up in Morgan's lap and she stroked her silky fur with one hand as she looked at the key with the other.

"I have no idea what this would go to. A trunk or another box?"

Fiona glanced over as she turned onto the road leading to Perkins cove. "I don't know. I mean what are the odds that whatever it opens is even in the attic?"

Morgan nodded. "But we really don't have any place else to try."

They made the rest of the short drive in silence and Celeste, Jolene and Cal were standing at the door when they pulled into their driveway.

Celeste and Jolene ran over and hugged them.

"I can't believe you guys got attacked!" Jolene said. "Are you all right?"

"Yes. Turns out we can take pretty good care of ourselves," Morgan said.

"But I'm still thankful Luke was there to pick up the pieces." Fiona winked at Morgan and she felt her cheeks grow warm.

"Let's see this key." Cal held out his hand and Morgan put the key in it.

"Oh yeah, this is an oldie." He held the long skeleton key up to the light, squinted at it then handed it back to Morgan.

"Jeez Cal, I hope we aren't keeping you from going to work. You don't have to watch over us day and night," Fiona said as they started up the main stairway.

"It's okay," he answered. "I have plenty of people to keep the shop running and I could use a little break. Plus I'll take any excuse to get back up into your attic and get my hands on all those antiques."

The girls laughed and Celeste swatted at him as they emerged into the attic.

Morgan stood at the top of the stairs and looked around.

"I have no idea where to start." She looked tentatively at Belladonna. She felt a little silly thinking the cat could show her the way, but Belladonna had led them to many important finds in the past.

This time, though, the cat simply curled up by the window, gave Morgan a blank stare and started cleaning herself.

"Follow your intuition, Morgan," Celeste said. "I

mean really dig deep and see if you get a feeling for where we should look."

Morgan took a deep breath and closed her eyes. She tried to focus on her feelings. *Was there a specific part of the attic that stood out?* She felt herself drawn toward an area in the very back and started moving toward it.

She stopped in front of a door and looked back at Cal and her sisters. "I think it's in here."

Her pulse kicked into high gear as she pushed the door open, the hinges squealing in the silent attic. Inside was a small room, probably ten feet by eight. It looked like it had once been one of the servants' rooms but now it held boxes stacked almost from floor to ceiling, along with haphazard piles of … stuff.

Cal walked over to one corner and started rummaging in a pile.

"These are really old," he said holding up a silver creamer and sugar.

"And look at this thing." Jolene pointed to long sword that stood against the wall.

Fiona had started looking through one of the trunks and Celeste rifled a pile of linens.

Morgan was busy sorting through a box of what looked like old pewter cups when she heard Fiona gasp.

She jerked her head in Fiona's direction. Her sister was sitting on the floor staring into a box.

"What is it?" Morgan shuffled over to see what was so interesting.

Fiona pulled what looked like a pile of burlap out of the box and laid it on the floor. Morgan's stomach flittered with butterflies as she watched her sister slowly open the flaps.

An array of gemstones and crystals lay inside. Morgan marveled at how they sparkled in the light and then her stomach squeezed when she realized the ones closest to Fiona were actually glowing.

"They're beautiful," Morgan said watching as Fiona reached for a brown stone in the corner. Morgan recognized it as tiger's eye—the same stone in the pendant Fiona had given her. Her hand flew up to the pendant and closed around it. It felt warm and she drew in a sharp breath when she saw the stone on the burlap glow as Fiona's hand touched it.

"What's that?" Celeste joined them.

"Old crystals." Fiona dropped the tiger's eye and looked up at them. "Well, all crystals are old, but these look like they have been here for centuries."

"They probably have, judging by the age of the other stuff in this room," Cal said.

"Looks like one of our ancestors was into crystals and gemstones, just like you," Jolene added.

"Yeah, I guess so." Fiona folded the burlap flaps back over the crystals and Morgan noticed the faint outline of printing on the material.

"Wait. What's that?" She pointed to the letters.

Fiona squinted down at it. "Looks like initials. MB. Guess I'll have to research who that was. Do you guys mind if I take these?"

No one minded. Fiona wrapped the crystals back up and the group got busy rummaging through the items. Morgan was just starting to feel like the whole exercise had been for nothing when she heard a sharp intake of breath from the other side of the room.

"Hey guys, I think I found something."

Jolene was crouched down in the corner, boxes pushed out of the way on either side of her. Morgan rushed over and looked down, her heart lurching up into her throat when she saw what had caused Jolene to call out.

There, on the floor in front of them was a box very similar to the other boxes they had found. Like the others, this one was silver, with gold on the corners and an ornate carved flower design. But it was much bigger—about a one and a half feet long and six inches wide. Morgan reached down and picked it up, her pulse picking up speed as she held it.

"Wowser. That's one nice box," Cal said.

"Does the key fit it?" Celeste asked.

Morgan found a table off to the side and put the box on top, then took the key out of her pocket.

She held her breath as she lined the key up with the hole in the lock. She inserted and turned. *Click.*

The top flew open. Inside was a long piece of leather, rolled up tight, the outside was dry and cracked with age.

"Be careful with that," Cal warned. "Old Leather can be very brittle."

She lifted the leather out and placed it on the table, then unrolled it very slowly. Her heart beat faster and faster as the images and writing inside were revealed.

It was a treasure map.

19

By the time they brought the map down to the informal living room, Jake had come home from work and joined them. They spread it out flat on the coffee table. Morgan inhaled the smell of old leather as she bent over to study the lines of the map which had been crudely burned into it.

"This looks like our yard, but it's shaped different," Jolene said.

"The geography of this area was changed about a hundred years ago, when the area started becoming attractive to tourists," Cal replied.

"Yeah, I remember reading about how the channel to the cove was made deeper and the cove itself much wider. Then on the other side, some land was filled in near Oarweed Cove where it abuts our land." Celeste pointed to the different parts of the map as she talked.

"So, our land as it sits now is here … and here?" Morgan drew a circle with her finger to indicate where she thought the land was.

"I think so," Cal said.

"So part of this isn't even our land."

"You're right … but the important part looks like it is." Cal pointed to the big X in the middle of the map where the supposed treasure was.

Morgan squinted at the map, it did look like the treasure was buried somewhere near the point of land at the edge of their property. Near where the body had been found.

She glanced outside. Plenty of daylight left. "We should start digg—"

The knock on the door interrupted her and she raised an eyebrow at the group.

"Anyone expecting company?"

Nobody was.

"We should hide this, just in case." She gestured to the map and Celeste and Jolene got busy rolling it up and finding a hiding spot. Morgan and Fiona went to answer the door that the insistent visitor was now pounding on.

"Hold your horses … I'm coming." She ripped

the door open and her heart froze when she saw who was standing there.

Sheriff Overton.

And he wasn't alone, he had several uniformed policemen with him and they looked like they were there for backup. But why would he need backup?

"Well 'bout time. I hope you aren't trying to hide any evidence because it's too late," Overton said with a smug smile on his face.

"What are you talking about?" Morgan stood feet apart, fists on her hips. She didn't invite Overton in, but he opened the screen door and stepped in anyway. The commotion had caused everyone else to gather in the hall.

"Oh good, I see you're all here. That will make it easy to arrest the killer."

Morgan's heart clenched. *What was he talking about?*

Fiona narrowed her eyes at the Sheriff. "No one invited you in, so you can turn around and leave."

"Oh, I don't think so. See, I got this little piece of paper here that says I got probable cause to bring the killer in for questioning."

The toothpick switched from one side of his mouth to the other as he pulled some papers from his front pocket and shoved them in Fiona's face.

Morgan felt her anger rising. "I already told you, I had nothing to do with killing that guy."

Overton looked at her and nodded. "Yep and, much to my surprise, you were telling the truth."

Morgan scrunched her face at him.

"It's not you I'm here to arrest … It's her." Overton pointed past Morgan's shoulder.

Her heart squeezed as she turned to follow the direction of his finger. It was pointing straight at Celeste.

"What!" Cal boomed, putting a protective arm around Celeste. "You can't just come in here and arrest people with no evidence."

"Oh, I have evidence." Overton smiled his Cheshire cat smile. "Found the murder weapon right in little Blondie's car."

"What are you talking about?" Morgan shot a glance at Celeste who looked as baffled as she was.

"Yep. The coroner got back to us this morning. The victim's head was bashed in with a round object … oh about this big." Overton cupped his hands to illustrate a circumference of about six or seven inches.

Morgan narrowed her eyes. "And you found one in Celeste's car?"

"Yep. Just happened to notice it when we were

here last night." He turned to one of the uniforms behind him. "Show her."

Morgan's eyes widened as the gangly kid held up a large plastic bag with one of Celeste's kettle bells inside.

"That handle makes 'em perfect for getting a good swing for bashing someone's head in, wouldn't you say?" Overton raised his eyebrows at Morgan.

"Those are for exercising!" Morgan louvered her eyes between Overton and Celeste. This had to be some sort of mistake or one of Overton's tricks.

"Let me see that." Jake pushed forward and grabbed at the paper Overton had shown to Fiona.

He glanced over it then looked at the kettle bell. "Is there forensic evidence on that?"

"We haven't run it through the lab yet but I'm sure it will prove to be the weapon." Overton stepped over toward Jake, taking the toothpick out of his mouth. "You better keep your nose out of this. In fact I think I'll put you on administrative leave until this case is over."

Jake opened his mouth to protest but Overton put his hand up to stop him.

"I should have you fired for consorting with known criminals," he said, jerking his chin toward Morgan and Celeste.

He turned to the uniforms behind him. "Now cuff her and take her away."

Cal stepped in front of Celeste. "Now wait just a minute!"

The uniforms froze and looked back at Overton uncertainly.

"Better step aside, Reed, or I'll have you brought in for obstruction of justice."

Celeste pushed in front of Cal, holding her wrists out together in front of her. "It's okay. I'll go with them and you guys can come and post bail. I'm not worried since I didn't kill anyone."

Morgan was impressed with her sister's calm demeanor.

It took everything she had to step aside while they cuffed Celeste and brought her out to the car, but she knew it was the best thing to do. As soon as they were gone, she'd be on the phone to the lawyer and working to get Celeste out of jail. There was nothing she could do right now to stop it, though, so she let them take her.

"We'll be down right behind you," she said to Celeste as they led her by.

Celeste nodded. "No hurry."

Morgan stood in the doorway, her fists clenched and the map all but forgotten as she watched them shove Celeste into the back of the police car and drive away.

She'd never felt so helpless in all her life.

* * *

"We have to get her out right away. I don't want her spending one night in there." Morgan turned to face the group, her mind whirling.

"I'll get on the phone to Delphine," Fiona said. Delphine Jones was the sharp witted lawyer they had used when Morgan had been accused of murder earlier in the summer. She'd done a fantastic job and Morgan couldn't think of anyone better to help Celeste.

"I'll put a call into some of my friends at the station." Jake whipped out his cell phone.

"We'll need money for a retainer," Morgan said.

"Don't worry about that," Cal replied. "I'll give you whatever you need for the lawyer."

"We're not taking your money."

"Consider it a loan, then. What you have in the attic is worth plenty of money … you can sell some of it later if you want, but for now I have cash at the ready and we don't want to hold up getting Celeste out."

Morgan nodded. He was right.

"Delphine's going to meet us down there," Fiona said as she headed out the door.

Morgan, Cal and Jolene followed. Jake stayed behind. His presence at the station wouldn't help things after the run in he'd just had with Overton.

Delphine Jones was already in the police station parking lot when they pulled up in Cal's pearl white Lincoln Navigator. She was on her cell phone, pacing back and forth in front of her car, arms gesturing wildly. Her hot pink jacket and pink, white and orange broom skirt fluttered in the breeze behind her.

She hung up when they pulled up next to her.

"Okay, give me the quick version." She tapped her nails on the hood of the Lincoln as Morgan told her how Celeste's kettle bells were the suspected murder weapon for the dead body on the cliff.

"Was there any evidence on the weapon?"

"Overton said they hadn't run them through the lab yet."

Delphine narrowed her eyes in the direction of the police station.

"Jerk." She spat the word out like it was sour yogurt.

Morgan knew from their previous dealings that there was no love lost between Delphine and the

Sheriff. She didn't know why but Overton seemed afraid of the feisty lawyer and Morgan knew that worked to their advantage.

"Can you get her out?" Fiona asked.

"Sure. Well, I might need a judge, especially if Overton is playing games with the murder weapon and delaying the testing. But I'll do my damn best to get her out tonight." They started off toward the police station entrance. "I'll go straight in to Overton and see if I can get him to release her and you guys can go down for a visit."

A blast of cool air hit Morgan as the entered the lobby and her stomach clenched remembering when *she* had been arrested. Delphine headed off to see Overton and Fiona demanded that they be allowed to visit Celeste.

Someone came out and led them down to the cells. Morgan's nerves grew more tense with each step. They filed past four empty cells, Celeste was in the last one—the same one Morgan had been in.

Morgan peered into the cell, her heart pounding wondering what kind of condition her sister was in.

Celeste sat on the bed, cross legged. Her eyes closed, breathing steady. She opened one eye then the other as a smile lit her face.

"Oh hi guys. You didn't have to come so fast," she

said as if they had dropped in for a leisurely Sunday afternoon visit.

"Celeste, are you okay? Did they hurt you?" Cal's face was lined with concern. Morgan narrowed her eyes at him, they were all concerned about Celeste but Cal seemed overly so. *What was up with that?*

"Oh I'm fine." She waved her hand. "It's not that bad here. The bed is comfortable and it's a great place to meditate ... very quiet and lots of emotional energy."

"We brought Delphine and she's going to get you out," Fiona said.

Celeste got up from the bed and came over to edge of the cell, looking out at them through the bars.

"I think I might be staying here tonight, but I don't want you guys to worry. I didn't kill that guy so I won't be here long. You need to focus on taking care of the guys that are after us ... I have it on good authority it's only going to get worse."

"What? You're not going to have to stay here," Jolene said.

"I'm afraid she is." Delphine came rushing toward them. "I need a judge to let her out and they've all gone home but I promise I'll get her out first thing in the morning."

Morgan felt like she'd been punched in the gut. "Seriously? But she didn't do anything."

"I know, sometimes the wheels of justice move backwards." Delphine patted Morgan's arm.

"It's okay, guys, really. Go—take care of things at home. Brandon's bringing me a lobster dinner and I'll be quite comfortable here." Celeste waved them off and Morgan saw Cal and her sisters reluctantly turn toward the door. Their tense faces echoing Morgan's worries.

They filed past Celeste, hugging her through the bars and saying good-bye. Delphine was already halfway down the hall when Morgan got her turn. Celeste grabbed her arm and held her back.

"Make sure you study that map. I don't know why you need to, but you do." Celeste's ice-blue eyes drilled into her own and Morgan felt an electrical current surge through her veins.

She nodded and Celeste let go of her arm. "Now get out of here … I'll see you tomorrow. Oh and Nana says be nice to your guest."

Morgan frowned at her. *Guest?* She was still wondering what Celeste meant when she climbed into Cal's car in the parking lot.

20

She didn't have to wonder for long.

Luke was waiting on the front porch when they got home. Sitting in the white wicker settee drinking a beer next to Jake, who was in one of the rockers. Making himself right at home.

Cal ran over and the two of them got reacquainted with the usual back slapping and hand shaking. They'd been friends before Luke left and, as far as Morgan knew, hadn't seen each other since.

Morgan's stomach flip-flopped as she approached the porch. Probably from all the excitement with Celeste, she reasoned. Surely it had nothing to do with how good Luke looked sitting on *her* porch drinking one of *her* beers.

"How did it go? Where's Celeste?" Jake stood

from his rocking chair, greeting Fiona with a peck on the cheek.

"Delphine couldn't get her out until tomorrow." Morgan felt her chest squeeze as she said it and she realized she was surprisingly close to tears.

Cal paced the porch. "Is there nothing we can do?"

"Short of going down with a nail file in a cake and breaking her out, I don't think so," Jake said. "She'll be okay. Is there anyone else in there?"

"The other cells were empty," Jolene replied.

"She'll be fine, we don't get too many criminals in there so she'll probably be alone … I guess I should say *they* don't since I'm officially on leave." Jake pressed his lips together. "Besides, my contact at the station assured me they'd treat her like a queen. Probably be like a vacation for her."

"Yeah, she did say someone named Brandon was bringing her lobster." Cal frowned.

Jake nodded. "That's Brandon Burchard. He'll take good care of her."

Morgan noticed Cal's frown deepen.

"Well, I don't know about the rest of you, but I could use a drink." Fiona reached for the door handle and everyone lined up behind her. Except Luke.

"Does someone want to fill me in on what's going on?" He frowned over his beer.

"Morgan will." Fiona shot over her shoulder as she went inside.

Morgan glanced at the door, then at Luke, her stomach flopping around like a fish out of water. They were alone on the porch.

Why did that make her so nervous?

Luke reached over and grabbed her hand, pulling her to the settee beside him.

"What's wrong, you look upset." He brushed a lock of hair behind her ear sending her pulse skittering like a frightened rabbit.

"Celeste got arrested for murder." Her voice cracked on the last word and the tears she felt sting her eyes earlier, threatened to spill out. It made her feel vulnerable. She hated feeling that way. She noticed that Luke had pulled her down close to him and she slid away to the other side of the settee. At least she could think better over there.

"Jake filled me in a little. He didn't tell me too much though. Probably didn't know how much he should tell me ... I guess he doesn't trust me fully." Luke turned his sea green eyes on her. "Do you?"

Morgan's breath caught in her throat. *Did she?*

"Well, you *have* helped us out of a few spots now.

But you've been gone for so long. I don't feel like I know you anymore." She picked at the wicker arm of the settee, avoiding his gaze.

"I'm the same person I always was. Just a little better traveled."

Morgan looked at him and realized he had slid a little closer to her. She pressed herself into the corner.

"Well, you'll excuse me if I'm not brimming over with trust. You disappeared out of my life ten years ago and I haven't heard a word from you since." Morgan tried to ignore the flutter in her stomach and act nonchalant, as if that was old news that barely affected her now.

He sighed and took a pull on his beer. Staring out at the ocean, he rubbed his dark short cropped hair which made it stick out as if he just got up. Out of bed. Morgan tried to push the memories of other times, when she'd seen his hair like that, out of her mind.

He put this beer down and turned to face her, his arm up on the back of the settee. She suddenly became very interested in studying her hands which were clasped in her lap.

"I didn't want to just walk out of your life. But I had to do what was right for you. It wasn't fair for me to expect you to wait for me." He put his thumb under her chin and gently turned her face toward him. "I thought about you every day."

Her heart squeezed in her chest. *Did he really?* She realized he'd slid over even closer to her. Suddenly, he was leaning toward her. She could smell the spicy scent of his after shave and feel the heat radiating from his body.

She flattened her palm on his chest to push him away, except she didn't push very hard. Beneath his thin shirt, she could feel hard muscle and the steady beat of his heart. She wondered if it was beating as fast as hers as she watched his lips get closer.

Before she knew what was happening, her eyes were drifting shut and his lips were brushing against hers. Tenderly at first, then pressing harder. She sighed and relaxed into his kiss.

"Meow!"

Belladonna jumped up onto Luke's lap and they jerked apart like two teenagers caught necking behind the rectory.

"Hey, this looks just like the cat you used to have." Luke reached down to pet the cat who had curled up in his lap and was staring up at him adoringly.

"It is."

Luke wrinkled his brow at her. "It's the same cat? She must be ancient by now."

Morgan bit her lip as she thought about that. How old *was* Belladonna? She'd had her since she was a kid, which would make the cat in her late teens.

How long did cats live, anyway?

Her stomach clenched thinking her cat might be nearing old age. She'd never thought much about it, but Belladonna had always been around—she didn't know what she'd do without her.

Morgan realized her earliest memories included the cat. That's impossible, she thought. It must have been a different cat. Her mother always doted on the cat and probably got another one that looked just like her when the first one passed.

Her thoughts were interrupted by the cat thwacking her arm with her tail as Luke petted her. She'd never heard Belladonna purr so loud.

"So anyway, tell me about the key, did you find the lock it fits in?"

Morgan took a deep breath and told him about the search in the attic and the leather map.

"In fact, we were trying to figure it out when Overton came to the door and arrested Celeste."

"Can I see the map?"

"Sure, it's right inside."

Luke dislodged Belladonna from his lap and she

grunted out a discontented "mew" as the two of them went inside.

"The map's in the informal living room. You remember where that is?"

Luke smiled that disarming smile he had and Morgan's stomach turned inside out.

Why did he have to be so damn handsome?

He started walking toward the room and she couldn't help but check him out. He'd always been tall and well built, but she could see that he'd put on some weight in the past ten years. And judging by what she'd felt through his tee-shirt, it was pure muscle.

Thinking of that reminded her of their brief kiss and she felt her cheeks heat up. She pushed away any of *those* type of thoughts about Luke before the heat could spread to other parts of her body.

It was just as well the cat had interrupted their kiss. She couldn't deny she was still attracted to Luke, but he'd be gone after this was all over and where would that leave her?

In the living room, the map had been spread out on the table again and everyone was discussing the various instructions so intently they barely noticed Luke and Morgan.

Jake glanced over. "Hey Luke, what do you make

of this? It says two steps as the crow flies. What does that mean?"

Luke rubbed the stubble on his chin. "Usually it means straight ahead without having to go around an obstacle."

"That's strange, there's no obstacle there." Jake pointed to a spot on the map then looked out the window.

"Well, sometimes they wrote up trick maps, or put the instructions in backwards or in code," Luke said. "In case the map fell into the wrong hands."

"I guess that explains why we dug the hole in the wrong place last time," Morgan said.

"That's right! I thought we had followed it wrong, but what really happened is that it was written backwards." Jolene pointed out the window to where they had dug up the box. "See how we were digging over there, but the box was found on the opposite side of the yard."

"So, do you think this map could be written backwards or in some sort of code?" Fiona raised a brow at Luke.

"It could be." He stared down at the map. "It's impossible to tell but the thing is you need to be really careful in case the treasure is booby trapped."

"Oh, that's right." Cal looked up at them, wide

eyed. "I had forgotten that pirates routinely did that. We could blow ourselves up."

"Not only that, but now that the pirates know you have the key and are getting close, I'm sure they are going to step up their efforts to try to get the treasure from you."

Morgan's heart squeezed. Luke was right, the danger was getting worse and there was no sign of it letting up. She knew she had to do something to stop it. She just wasn't sure exactly what.

"I'm not sure I like the way things are heading —we need to be proactive instead of waiting for them to attack us," Fiona echoed Morgan's thoughts.

"What prompted Overton to arrest Celeste?" Luke asked.

"He was poking around in her car and saw something the same shape as the murder weapon," Fiona replied

"And what was that?"

"Kettle bells."

"Huh?" Luke cocked an eyebrow at her.

"They're like weights for exercising, but they have a handle and a round ball on the bottom. You kind of swing them around." Jolene made swinging motions with her arms.

Luke ruffled his hair and looked out the window. After a few seconds he turned back to the group

"Are they about this big?" He cupped his hands making about a seven inch circle.

"Yes!"

He nodded then did more staring out the window.

"Okay, I think I have an idea that might help us get the treasure hunters off your back *and* give Overton the real murder weapon, which will clear Celeste and put the real killer in jail." He looked around the group, staring each of them directly in the eye in turn.

"But I'm going to need one of you to act as a decoy."

21

Morgan felt bats flapping around in her stomach as everyone stared at Luke in silence.

A decoy? That sounded dangerous.

"I'll do it," she blurted out.

Luke narrowed his eyes at her. "Morgan it could be dangerous."

Duh.

"No, it should be me," Jake volunteered.

"Or me," Cal added.

Luke sighed. "It has to be one of the girls. Otherwise *I'd* do it. The treasure hunters won't bite if it's a guy. They'll be expecting it to be one of the Blackmoore sisters and … well … they won't be as intimidated by a woman."

"Well, that settles it, then. I'll be the decoy. I'm not letting Fiona or Jolene do it." Morgan's mind was made up.

Luke raised his hands in a gesture of defeat. "I guess you're right. I don't like it, but there's no other way."

"So what do I do?"

"I need you to lure the treasure hunters out into the open. I haven't been able to get the ones we captured to talk and I can't figure out where the rest of them are hiding. I think they are on those boats you guys saw, but they could be docking them anywhere and they're probably moving them around all the time."

"I'm not sure I like the sounds of this." Fiona narrowed her eyes at Luke.

"Me either," he said. "But they know you guys are getting close and I think they realize they won't have many more chances. They'll probably send most of their guys considering what's happened the last two times. All I need is for Morgan to pretend like she has some sort of a lead and that will get them swarming."

"What do you mean?" Jake asked.

"We know they are watching because they were on Morgan and Fiona pretty quick today when they dug up the key. So, I'm thinking that Morgan can act like she's onto the treasure or has another clue and start digging. I figure if we do it at *Sticks and Stones* we won't lead them to the real treasure here." Luke turned to look at Morgan. "And if Morgan is alone, she'll make an easy target."

Morgan's stomach clenched but she straightened her back. She wasn't one to back down from a challenge. "Okay. Let's go."

"Well, hold on. I need to put my men in place. We'll be watching you every second, of course, and I'm also going to have you wear a wire so we can hear you and rush in as soon as possible. That will be the safest way. I could never forgive myself if anything happened to you."

Morgan's heart melted at the tender look in Luke's eyes.

"So we'll do it tomorrow," He said then turned to the rest of the group, "if everyone agrees."

"Only if you're sure Morgan won't get hurt." Jolene's blue eye's challenged Luke.

"I won't let anything happen to her."

Jolene nodded. "Okay by me, then."

"I guess we don't have much of a choice," Fiona said. "The sooner we can get this all over with the better."

"Agreed," Jake said and Cal nodded.

"Okay then, I better get things going," Luke said. "I'm going to leave through the side door over by the Cove, I can use the cover of the hedges in case the bad guys are watching … we don't want to tip them off that we've been planning anything."

"I'll show you out." Morgan heard herself say then convinced herself that it wasn't that she wanted to be alone with him—it was the polite thing to do.

They crossed the hallway and went through the kitchen to the butler's pantry that led to the side door.

The small area on this side of the house had been one of Morgan's favorite places since childhood. It was like a secret garden. A rounded trellis covered in pink roses framed the door, colorful flowers sprouted up on either side and two honeysuckle bushes sent a sweet perfume through the air.

The shrubs, about ten feet away, enclosed the area in a private cocoon and a wrought iron bench with a stuffed canvas cushion tucked away under a large oak tree made a perfect place for reading.

Morgan stood on the top step and Luke a step down, his eyes level with hers.

"Are you sure you're okay doing this?" Luke's had caught her by the wrist and her heart skipped a beat.

"Yeah, of course. We need to do *something*, right?" She shrugged.

Luke looked thoughtful for a few seconds and Morgan felt a warm summer breeze flirt with her cheek. It was dusk, that magical moment when the daylight fades and the moonlight takes over. She could smell the flowery perfume of the honeysuckle and hear the summer peepers cheeping away.

How many other nights had she and Luke spent listening to peepers in the dusk?

She could feel the heat where his hand encircled her wrist and was suddenly intensely aware of him. She saw indecision in his eyes and then they turned dark with desire. His hand left her wrist and he wrapped it in her hair as he pulled her toward him.

She didn't resist.

Even though she knew she should.

Instead she met his lips eagerly, her arms snaking around his neck, her body pressing closer to his.

His lips were warm and tasted sweetly salty. They were familiar, but different somehow. She briefly wondered how many other women had tasted those lips in the past ten years as Luke's arm encircled her waist pulling her in even closer.

The feel of his hands on her body sent tiny frissons of pleasure shooting through her, reawakening the passion that had lain dormant all these years.

* * *

LUKE CURLED his hand around Morgan's soft, silky hair as she responded to his kisses, heating his veins with passion. He let his hand fall to her slim waist, her hips and then down her backside.

He pulled her hard against him and her moan of pleasure almost brought him to the brink of no return.

He shouldn't be kissing her like this, but he couldn't help it. In the past ten years he hadn't met anyone else that could even come close to matching his feelings for Morgan.

He was beginning to question why he ever left here in the first place, and, in the back of his mind, was already coming up with a plan for sticking around after this was all over.

But first, he had to do whatever he could to make sure Morgan was safe tomorrow and that was going to take a lot of thinking and planning. Which meant he better stop kissing her ... while he could still think.

Reluctantly, he pulled away.

Looking at her in the twilight, his heart flipped in his chest at how beautiful she was. Her raven colored hair shone in the moonlight. He brushed a silky strand away from her face and gazed into her half closed ice-blue eyes. Desire burned in his veins as his thumb traced the line of her bottom lip, all pouty and swollen from their kiss.

He fought off the urge to pull her close and kiss her again. He knew this time he wouldn't be able to stop, so he stepped away, plunging his hands into the pockets of his cargo pants.

"You don't have to do this, you know ... the decoy thing tomorrow, I mean. I can figure out another way to get rid of the treasure hunters."

He hoped she'd change her mind and decide not to, but he knew she wouldn't. He would have called the whole thing off but he also knew how stubborn she could be and figured she'd do something crazy on her own—especially if it helped prove Celeste wasn't the killer. It was better to follow through with his plan so he could keep an eye on her.

Luke saw her dreamy half closed eyes snap wide open and her back stiffen. "No, I want to do it. I'm not afraid of some old pirates. Don't even think about trying to talk me out of it."

Luke took his hands out of his pockets, spreading them wide. "I wouldn't dream of it. But I want to make sure you're comfortable with doing this ... and I also want to make sure you don't get hurt."

He reached out, running his fingers lightly down

her arm. He could see suspicion lurking behind her narrowed eyes.

Better quit while you're ahead.

He backed away, his heart squeezing tighter with each step. He suddenly felt like a schoolboy after his first kiss, not knowing the right thing to say. He cleared his throat, taking another backwards step.

"I'll be here first thing tomorrow then … to let you know the exact plan."

Morgan nodded. "Okay."

Then he turned his heart pounding as he disappeared through the shrubs. The job he had ahead of him was probably the most important one he'd ever had. He had to make sure the plan was perfect … his whole future depended on it.

MORGAN STARED at Luke's retreating back and kicked herself for falling under his spell so easily. Her fingers flew to her lips that were still burning from his kiss.

He'd sure kissed her like he meant it, but what Morgan couldn't figure out was why? The past ten years had made it perfectly clear that he didn't have room for her in his life and she certainly had no intention of being just a passing dalliance.

Her hand closed around the cold metal of the doorknob. Better to get on with the task at hand than to stand there wondering. The sooner all this pirate stuff was over with, the sooner Luke Hunter would be gone from her life—hopefully this time for good.

But right now she had something more important to do.

She slipped inside to the butler's pantry and made her way to the informal living room. She was glad to find it empty—she didn't want to answer any embarrassing questions about her and Luke tonight.

The map was still laid out on the table. She sat down on the couch to study it. Celeste's parting words echoed in her head and she was learning that it was smart to follow Celeste's advice.

Staring down at the lines in the map, she realized something wasn't quite right. The map was a series of markers with lines leading from one to the next and some sparse instructions. Presumably you would follow the lines and find the treasure at the end.

But, something about the lines wasn't right—she could feel it in her gut. Morgan closed her eyes and pictured the map in her mind. It seemed to float, almost three dimensionally as if the map was drawn for terrain that was at different elevations instead of a straight line on flat ground.

A sudden sound in front of her made her heart lurched. Her eyes flew open, her body tensing.

She relaxed when she saw it was only Belladonna. The cat had hopped up on the table and sat on the map, her tail swishing over the corner of it, blue eyes staring intently at Morgan.

Morgan remembered how the cat threw herself at Luke earlier.

"Traitor."

Belladonna simply blinked at Morgan, licked her paw, washed her ear a couple of times then continued staring.

Morgan returned her attention to the map, studying it as she was instructed. Belladonna sat patiently on the table and Morgan couldn't help but wonder if the cat knew something she didn't.

Morgan could feel her eyes growing heavy. It had been a long day and an even longer one was in store tomorrow. Her chest constricted at the thought of being a decoy, but she *had* to do it—her family was being threatened and if she could make it go away then it was worth the risk.

She wandered into the kitchen and made a cup of chamomile tea to help her sleep.

Where was everyone?

A quick glance at the clock told her it was late— they were probably in bed. And that's exactly where she should be, trying to get a good night's sleep. She'd need her wits about her tomorrow to deal with the bad guys … and Luke Hunter.

22

M organ was up early the next day, anxiety seeping into her every pore, making her jumpy and jittery. She hadn't slept well, but figured coffee was a bad idea so she padded down to the kitchen in her bare feet, black tank top and favorite pair of faded jeans for some tea.

Fiona, Cal, Jake and Jolene were quietly sitting at the kitchen island staring into steaming mugs of coffee.

"I guess I'm not the only one up early," Morgan said as she hunted in the cabinet for her favorite mug.

"Yeah who can sleep with Celeste in jail and you acting as some sort of decoy?" Fiona raised a sleepy eyebrow.

Morgan shrugged. "I'm sure I'll be fine, and Delphine will get Celeste out today."

"Yeah, we're going to meet her in a little bit," Cal said looking at his watch.

Morgan's heart thumped. They were all going off to get Celeste out of jail and she'd be going off to get captured by pirates.

"Morgan will be perfectly safe and under our watchful eye with these gadgets," Luke said from the kitchen doorway as if reading her mind.

Everyone swiveled in his direction. He was dressed in a black tee-shirt that somehow managed to show off every muscle in his chest and arms along with black cargo pants and big steel toed boots, also in black.

Morgan's heart thumped even harder. "How did you get in here?"

"Oh, sorry, I snuck in. Didn't want to come to the front door in case anyone was watching." Luke shrugged. "I wasn't kidding when I said you guys should get an alarm system."

Morgan narrowed her eyes at him, taking in the three small items he was holding in his hand.

"What are those?"

"These are your lifeline. This will allow us to see everything going on around you." He held up what looked like a barrette in his right hand.

"And these will let us hear everything." He held

up a pair of earrings in his left.

Jolene went over to inspect the items. "These are pretty cool. Unobtrusive. Do they really work?"

"Like a charm. You wanna try them out?"

"I'd love to. Actually I was hoping I could kind of tag along and see how the whole process works."

Luke frowned at her.

"I'm taking some private investigator courses and a computer forensics course. It would be really helpful for me to see some real life stuff." Morgan noticed that she was giving Luke that wide-eyed look she always gave Morgan whenever she wanted to talk her into something. Apparently it worked on Luke too.

Luke pursed his lips. "Okay, but don't be alarmed by my men—they can be kind of gruff. And don't get in the way."

"I won't. I've seen gruff guys before." Jolene winked at him.

Morgan realized there was a whole bunch she didn't know about her little sister.

Luke crossed the room and leaned against the counter next to Morgan who focused on sipping her tea while trying not to notice how good he smelled … or looked.

"Okay, so here's how we're going to do this. We'll set Morgan up with the camera and audio. I have several guys in strategic locations and we can monitor her on these." He reached into his cargo pants and pulled out a small tablet.

"That looks like an iPad." Jolene craned her neck to check out the device.

"It's very similar but specialized for surveillance work."

"Cool."

"I'll also be watching Morgan directly with high powered binoculars as will a couple of my associates. We should be able to see and hear everything and rush in as soon as the other guys try to grab her."

Morgan took a deep breath, setting down her mug. "Well, it all sounds very simple and easy. When do we get started?"

Luke looked at his watch. "What time do you usually open the shop?"

"Around eight."

"You should go there like normal. Open the shop and then walk around out back in the woods like you are looking for something. Maybe it would be a good idea to take a piece of paper, like you are following a map. Bring a shovel like you did the other day and start digging." Luke shrugged. "Then just let things happen."

"We better run." Fiona got up from her chair and hugged Morgan. "Good luck."

Morgan's heart squeezed and her stomach felt heavy with dread. She shook off the brief thought that this could be the last time she talked to her sisters.

"Thanks. Say hi to Celeste for me."

Cal and Jake hugged Morgan, then slapped Luke on the back and filed out.

Luke looked at Jolene. "You can come with me. But you need to change into all black so you'll be less noticeable."

Jolene's eye lit up and she jumped off her chair.

"I have just the outfit." She raced out of the room leaving Morgan and Luke alone.

Morgan feigned interest in her mug of tea, her heart racing like an overwound toy.

Luke moved closer to her, holding the earrings and barrette. "Let me help you get these on."

"I can do it." She grabbed the items, accidentally brushing his hand with hers, sending sparks running up her arm.

Her hands were shaking as she stabbed the earrings at the holes in her ears.

Luke leaned back, hands crossed over his chest

with an amused look on his face as she rammed the barrette into her hair.

"It's crooked," he said, reaching over to straighten it. He let his hand linger, then ran his fingers down the length of her hair all the while moving closer and looking at her with those damn sea green eyes.

He leaned in. Was he going to kiss her? Did she want him to?

Morgan's heart jerked in her chest, either from the task ahead of her or the closeness of Luke. She didn't know which. But either way, kissing him wasn't on her agenda this morning.

She backed away, ignoring the look of disappointment and confusion in his eyes.

"Let's get this over with." She grabbed her purse and headed for the door.

MORGAN'S PULSE raced as she punched in the security code at *Sticks and Stones*. The hairs on the back of her neck prickled. She knew Luke and his men were watching … but who else was?

Inside the shop seemed unusually quiet. Every creak and groan of the old floorboards set Morgan's heart skittering. She wasn't used to being alone in the shop and she felt a heavy weight in the pit of her stomach wishing Fiona was there with her.

She puffed her cheeks and blew out a long breath of air.

Better get to it.

Digging in her purse, she pulled out a piece of paper that would serve as her fake map and made her way to the back door. The trowel she used the day before was still leaning against the cottage and she grabbed it then headed off into the woods.

Morgan's heart raced as she wound her way through the trees, pretending like she was following instructions on the map. She clutched at the pendant Fiona had given her the day before. It felt warm, pulsating with energy.

Holding the paper in front of her, she walked east a few paces, then turned and walked north. The woods that always seemed so friendly and inviting took on a dark and foreboding air. Every noise set her nerves on edge.

A movement to her left set her heart jerking wildly. She whipped her head around and sighed when she realized it was only a squirrel scurrying up a tree.

She stopped at a giant pine that looked like it had been there for centuries. Squatting down, she placed the map on the ground next to her and cleared away the leaves and pine needles before shoving the trowel into the dirt.

Her heart was beating so loudly she wondered if Luke could hear it in the audio. Surely he could hear her raspy breath and see her shaky hands as she dug.

She tried to push away the heavy feeling of doom that was growing in the pit of her stomach. The bad guys would come then Luke would rush in and capture them and it would all be over. At least that was what was supposed to happen. But why did she *feel* like there wasn't going to be a happy ending?

A movement to her right caught her attention.

Another squirrel?

Then a movement behind her caused her to jerk her head in that direction. Her heart exploded in her chest when she saw them rushing at her from all directions. She bolted up and tried to run but strong, hairy arms grabbed her.

Morgan struggled, kicking out, trying to wriggle out of his grasp. Her eyes darted around frantically.

Where was Luke?

Her nose twitched as it was struck by a cloyingly sweet smell. She saw a red bandana rushing up to her face. She tried to jerk her head away, but the hairy paw held it in place as the bandana covered her nose and mouth.

Morgan's eyes bulged, her lungs gasped for fresh air.

Her struggles grew weaker.

And then, everything went black.

* * *

LUKE JABBED at the buttons on the tablet in frustration.

Why wasn't this thing working?

He'd seen Morgan go into the shop, but once she was inside, the video feed had turned to static. He couldn't hear the audio either, but that was probably because she wasn't saying anything.

"Is something wrong?" Jolene peered over his shoulder.

"This feed isn't working right." Luke turned the display on the tablet toward her.

Jolene looked at it then glanced through the shrubs toward *Sticks and Stones.*

"Electromagnetic interference," she said.

"What?" Luke wrinkled his brow at her.

"There's something weird going on at Sticks and Stones. I'm not sure if it's the building or the land but every time I go there I feel a surge of energy. My hair gets all staticy and stands on end. It's weird." Jolene turned to face him. "If there was some strange energy field there, would that interfere with your device?"

Luke pursed his lips together. An electromagnetic energy field? It seemed rather farfetched, but then some of the other things going on around the Blackmoore sisters were pretty farfetched so why should this be any different?

"I suppose it could."

Luke tapped on his headset to communicate with the rest of the team. "Does anyone have a good display?"

He got five negative responses.

"So no one can see or hear what's going on?"

More negative responses.

"Anyone have a visual with binocs?"

"I think she's still inside. I'm looking at the back door," a voice replied in his ear.

Luke grabbed his binoculars and trained them on the cottage. They were situated about one eighth mile away, on a ridge behind some shrubs facing the south end.

He didn't see anyone.

He jabbed at his tablet again, his stomach

clenching when neither the visual or sound worked. If he couldn't see or hear Morgan, then she could be in real danger.

"There she is," a voice in his ear announced and Luke picked up the binoculars again. This time, he could see Morgan come out the back door of the shop with a piece of paper in hand. He watched her grab a trowel and head off to the east.

Beside him, Jolene raised her binoculars, pointing them in the same direction as his.

He scanned the woods, looking for movement.

No one else was near.

He turned the binoculars back on Morgan just in time to see her turn and disappear behind a tree.

"Shit," Jolene muttered beside him.

The thick tree trunk blocked their line of vision. Morgan must have been traveling straight north because Luke couldn't see her at all.

He glanced down at the tablet, his heart thudding against his ribcage. It was mostly static, but he could see flashes of video now.

The woods looked clear.

Another flash of video and the angle changed, as if Morgan was bending down. In the next flash, he saw the trowel move toward the dirt.

Luke alternated between the binoculars and the tablet, his muscles tense, heart racing.

And then he saw an explosion of activity from several places in the woods. His heart lurched in his chest as he saw the men were dangerously close to Morgan. He dropped the tablet and binoculars and burst out of his hiding spot, heading straight for the woods as he gave the command on his headset.

"Go! Go! They've got her!"

As he ran toward the woods, his heart sank to his stomach. The static on the video had caused them to miss the bad guys' arrival and had given them an advantage. He hadn't planned on letting them get anywhere near Morgan, and now it looked like they'd gotten very close.

He burst into high gear, his legs pumping faster than they ever had.

He didn't know if the GPS tracker on his devices would work with all the static interference and he had to get to Morgan before they took her anywhere, otherwise he might not be able to track her.

He just hoped he wasn't already too late.

23

M organ slowly drifted out of the darkness to consciousness. Her back pressed against something hard and damp. Her nostrils stung with the sharpness of the salty sea air. She opened her eyes for a second then had to squeeze them shut to fight a wave of nausea.

Where was she?

Through half opened eyes she saw that it was dark, wherever she was, but she could see a light a few feet away. Some sort of lantern. She opened her eyes all the way. Above her was solid black, no stars or moon.

She was inside somewhere … no, not inside —*underground*.

She rolled to a sitting position, thankful the

nausea seemed to be disappearing. Her pulse quickened as she looked around. She was in some sort of
cave. The walls were rock and the floor hard,
compacted dirt. It was damp and smelled of the sea
—was she below sea level?

The room, if you could call it that, was big with a
few empty crates in the middle and a large iron door
that was set into a stone opening on one end. She
could see a tunnel and flickering light through the
open bars. Her heart stuttered when she saw iron
chains bolted unto large metal plaques in the stone
wall in various places around the room.

Was she in an old pirates' dungeon?

She heard voices coming from the direction of
the iron door and her blood turned cold.

Was it the men who captured her?

What did they want with her?

She could hear them laughing and her nerves
zinged with anxiety as the voices drew closer.

"Oh, I see you're awake." A large man with an
unruly red beard unlocked the padlock on the door
and came into the room along with another dark
haired man.

Morgan backed up as they approached her. Red
beard stopped about a foot from her. He smelled like
he hadn't bathed in a month and she could see

crumbs in his beard. Her stomach turned over and she tried not to gag.

"What do you want?" She tried to make her voice sound strong and powerful, but it came out in more of a squeak.

The two men looked at each other and laughed.

"We want to know where the treasure is," dark hair said stepping a little closer.

"I don't know where it is." Morgan touched her earrings, wondering if Luke could hear what was going on. *Do these things work in caves?* She tilted her head to the side so the barrette faced the two men, just in case.

"Sure you do. You found the map by now, didn't you? The real map I mean, not that fake one you had when we nabbed you."

Morgan's heart squeezed and she thought about the leather map. She hesitated too long before answering which set off more laughter. Then red beard got right in her face and his eyes weren't laughing or smiling—they were hard and cold. Her blood froze in her veins.

"No more games now. You're going to show us what's on the map or that young sister of yours is going to have a very bad day."

Morgan's heart clenched. "What do you mean? Have you done something to her?"

Black hair laughed. "Not yet, but if you don't give us what we want, she'll wish she was never born."

Red beard looked at black hair out of the corner of his eye. "Yeah and she's just your type isn't she?"

The two men laughed lewdly and Morgan remembered Celeste's warning to memorize the map. Could this be why? Was she *supposed* to tell them where the treasure was?

"If I tell you what's on the map, how do I know you still won't hurt my sister?"

"You don't, but you also don't have any choice, so you might as well spill or we'll let you watch us hurt all of your sisters before we do the same to you."

Morgan's heart dropped in her chest. She didn't have much of a choice and drawing them a map would buy her time and hopefully in that time Luke would be able to find her and dispense with the bad guys.

"Okay, I'll draw it for you."

Red beard produced paper and a pencil and Morgan used one of the boxes as a surface for the drawing. She contemplated drawing the map wrong, but her gut feeling told her to go with what was exactly on the leather map as she had memorized it.

When she was done, she handed him the paper. "Are you going to let me go now?"

The two men laughed.

"Do you think we're stupid? We're going to check this out and then … *maybe* we'll let you go," he said then glanced down at the paper. "Unless you tried to trick us with a fake map. Then we'll come back and make you wish you hadn't."

Morgan shivered at his words, rubbing her upper arms as the men turned to leave. She watched them slam the iron door shut and lock it then listened to their retreating footsteps echo off the walls.

As soon as they were out of earshot, she ran over to the door. She pushed. She pulled. It wouldn't budge. She looked down at the lock, remembering how Jolene had popped the lock on the box with a hairpin in the attic. It wasn't the same kind of lock but she took the barrette out of her hair and tried anyway. The only thing she succeeded in doing was mangling the barrette.

Morgan pressed her back against the wall, her stomach sinking like a lead ball. She was trapped. She slid down the wall, to a sitting position and put her face in her hands.

"Mew."

What was that?

Morgan jerked her head up and looked toward the iron door. Nothing was there.

"Meeew." More insistent this time, but the cave like walls acted as an echo chamber and she couldn't tell where it was coming from.

"Meeeooow."

That sounded just like Belladonna.

Morgan stood up, swiveling her head from side to side. She walked to the far end of the room, the one that was furthest away from the lantern. Her eyes adjusted to the darkness and she saw the cat sitting near one of the chains that hung from the wall.

"Where did you come from?" Morgan bent down to pet her. She must have snuck in through the bars of the door when Morgan had her head in her hands.

Did that mean Luke was coming?

The cat weaved her way around Morgan's ankles, then headed over toward the wall.

"Meow."

Morgan looked over. The cat was in front of a giant iron plaque that held in one of the chains that came out of the wall.

Then suddenly, she was gone!

Then back again.

Belladonna was going in and out of a big hole in the wall just behind the plaque!

Morgan rushed over and poked her head in. It looked like there was some kind of passageway or tunnel behind there. Too bad the opening was only big enough for her head.

If she could just move the plaque a little more …

She pushed, but it didn't budge.

Belladonna poked her head out of the opening. "Meeeooow!"

"Okay, okay. I'm trying."

Morgan braced herself against the floor and pushed on the plaque with her feet.

It moved an inch.

She pushed harder.

Another inch.

She pulled back her leg and kicked out with all her might and the plaque slid about six inches. Just enough to fit her body through.

Belladonna poked her head out again, then turned around and flicked her tail as if for Morgan to follow.

Morgan took one backwards glance at the room then wriggled through the hole into the tiny tunnel on the other side.

* * *

THE SMELL of rotting seaweed and dead fish made her want to vomit. Morgan had to crawl on her hands and knees as the tunnel wasn't big enough to stand in. The bottom was slimy and she shuddered to think what that slime was. Every so often her fingers would touch something squishy and her stomach churned wondering what icky creatures lived there.

It was dark in the tunnel. She could barely see Belladonna's white tail, like a flag, waving in front of her. As she crawled along behind it, she realized she had no idea where she was.

Underground somewhere, but where?

And how *far* underground?

The smell of the ocean was strong, so she figured she must be on the coast, but that could be a dozen places near where she was captured. She realized she had no idea how long she was unconscious—they could have taken her anywhere.

It seemed like she was going uphill—hopefully toward the surface. She'd had about enough of the damp underground.

The passage got increasingly larger until she could almost stand up. Her hands and knees were bruised and bleeding from crawling so she stood as best she could. She still had to bend over a little, but walking upright was much faster.

After a minute or two, she noticed it was getting brighter in the tunnel as if there was an opening not too far ahead. At least she hoped that's what it was. She picked up the pace.

Suddenly Belladonna stopped short in front of her. Morgan felt the floor beneath her shake. She heard a strange rumbling sound.

Belladonna looked back at her then started forward at a trot.

Morgan did the same, her heart beating wildly against her chest as she noticed small rocks becoming dislodged from the sides and top of the passage.

Bang!

The explosion rocked the passage. Morgan watched in horror as the walls and ceiling seemed to cave in before her eyes.

Her heart seized as she looked in front of her just in time to see a large rock hit Belladonna. The cat fell, then sprang up again but Morgan could see more rocks heading toward her.

Without thinking, she threw herself on top of Belladonna to shield the small cat from the onslaught of rocks. Two seconds later, the entire tunnel collapsed burying them both.

* * *

So this is what it's like to be buried alive.

The stones and dirt lay heavy on Morgan, pressing the air out of her lungs as she waited to die. She could hear voices and wondered if they were spirits welcoming her to 'the other side'. Maybe her mother and grandmother would be there. She wondered if she'd come back as a ghost and start talking to Celeste.

The voices were getting louder, the air in her lungs getting smaller.

Was the pile on top of her getting lighter, or was that her spirit departing?

She could hear rocks scraping, then she felt someone tugging at her arms.

"I've got her!"

Was that Luke?

Morgan tried to open her eyes as she felt the pile being cleared away on top of her. Strong arms tried to turn her over. Someone brushed the hair away from her face.

"Morgan, can you hear me?"

She nodded then slitted her eyes open. Luke's face was hovering above her, his eyes clouded with concern. He reached down and tenderly touched her face.

"Let's get you out of here," he said scraping at the rest of the rocks.

Morgan's heart lurched when she remembered Belladonna. The cat was right underneath her, but she didn't feel her moving.

Her heart dropped. *Was Belladonna dead?*

Tears stung her eyes as she wriggled free from the debris, looking underneath where she had been for a sign of the cat but there was none.

Luke pulled her the rest of the way out and took her in his arms, kissing her face, her lips, her forehead. Jolene was hugging her from behind. But Morgan was still thinking about the cat.

"Wait." Morgan pushed away from them and they looked at her with alarm.

"Belladonna is still in there, she may be hurt." Morgan practically sobbed out the words.

"What are you talking about?" Jolene raised an eyebrow at her. "She's sitting right here."

Morgan looked over to where Jolene was pointing. Belladonna sat on the grass next to the rubble-filled hole Morgan had just come out of, her fur white as snow, no sign of injury, calmly licking her paw as if it was just another regular day.

Morgan felt a surge of relief run through her

body as Belladonna looked up at her with big ice-blue eyes.

And then, she could have sworn, the darn cat winked at her.

EPILOGUE

Two days later, Morgan settled into the most comfortable chair in the informal living room, a cup of tea in her hand and Belladonna in her lap. Somehow she'd only sustained minor cuts when the tunnel caved in on her and those were bandaged along with some small carnelian stones Fiona had shoved in under the gauze.

"How did you figure out what the *real* murder weapon was?" Fiona looked at Luke who hovered around Morgan making sure her tea cup was full and her bandages were secure.

"That was easy. When I heard the description of the kettle bells, I knew that it matched the size and shape of old cannon balls. And what better thing for a pirate treasure hunter to use to bash in a rivals skull than an old cannon ball?" He spread his hands.

"Then once we found the bad guys' boats, it was easy to get on board and find the actual cannon ball that did it. We figure the treasure hunters from one group must have killed him on their boat and put him on the cliff as a warning to the members of the other group."

"I'm just glad you could turn all that over to Overton and get Celeste cleared," Cal said.

"And put the group of pirates that didn't blow themselves up in jail so we won't have to worry about them anymore," Jolene added.

"Well, Overton didn't seem very happy about the evidence. He seemed rather disappointed, but he couldn't argue with it. The two rival groups kind of helped us since they were getting in the way of each other's efforts. Thankfully they have both now been neutralized," Luke said.

"Too bad it took blowing up half our yard to do it." Celeste jerked her chin toward the window and Morgan felt her stomach clench as she looked outside.

The yard was about twenty feet shorter now. A giant half-moon shaped crater had been blown out of the cliff facing the Atlantic during the explosion which had caused the tunnel on the other end of the yard, that Morgan had been in, to cave in. Luckily she'd been near the surface. Otherwise she might not be sitting here today. She shivered and scratched Belladonna behind the ears.

The cat had saved her.

"That old treasure was booby-trapped just like you said it might be." Morgan looked up at Luke. "I guess I got lucky that I was far enough away. I'm still not sure exactly how you found me, though."

"You can thank Jolene for that," Luke said. "The tracking devices didn't work because of some strange interference at *Sticks and Stones* so I didn't see the treasure hunters sneak in. I tried to run over there when they grabbed you, but I wasn't fast enough. Jolene was the one who figured out to watch the road and then we knew which direction they took you in."

Morgan looked at Jolene, her heart swelling with pride. "Thanks."

Jolene laughed. "Well, I guess those private investigator classes are paying off."

"And then Jake was smart enough to take a dinghy out from the cove and he noticed the tunnel in the cliff. It's just above the low tide mark so it's underwater most of the time ... or well it was until it got blown up. They must have been planning to grab you right at low tide to get you in there the whole time."

Morgan's stomach churned remembering the

dank ocean smell inside the tunnel. No wonder the smell was so strong.

"Then the GPS in the barrette started working and we were practically on top of you when the explosion happened." Luke looked out the window. "There must be a warren of caves and passages out there if they brought you in on the side of the cliff and you came out down by the end of your driveway."

Morgan remembered the room she had been in with the iron door. There was a passage leading to it, presumably the one from the cliff, and then the tunnel that she crawled out of. She hadn't seen any sign of other passages but it was certainly possible.

She was just glad she was out of there, safe and sound with her family.

"It sounds like you guys did some awesome team-work to find me. I'm really overwhelmed and grateful," she said, tears pricking the backs of her eyes. "It was scary down there."

"We did work pretty good together," Jake said, "which helped me make an important decision."

Morgan's eyes widened. "Oh, really?"

"Yes. I'm quitting the police force and going into private investigation. Jolene is going to work with me."

"Oh, that's wonderful!" Morgan was genuinely pleased. "Are you sure you won't miss Overton too much?"

Everyone laughed.

"Not in the least." Jake winked at Morgan. "Although I am sorry I won't be there to keep you girls company when you get arrested."

Morgan widened her eyes in mock consternation and Celeste swatted at Jake playfully.

"Well, that works out good for me then," Luke said.

"And why is that?" Jake narrowed his eyes at him.

"Well …" Luke looked hesitantly at Morgan and her stomach flip flopped. *What was he up to?*

"I might have to hire you because I'm going to be needing some extra help … since I'm going to be spending less time traveling and more time right here in Noquitt." Morgan's heart thumped loudly against her ribcage as he put his hand over hers.

"Well, I'm glad everyone is safe and the pirates won't be bothering us anymore. I was kind of hoping we could recover the treasure, but now I guess it's been blown to smithereens." Fiona gazed out the window.

"You have plenty of treasure right up in your attic. Just these boxes alone are worth a lot of money." Cal gestured to the silver box in the table in front of Morgan that had contained the map.

Morgan picked it up. It *was* a beautiful box—Cal had verified it was solid sterling silver with 20k gold edging. Worth a lot just for the metal content alone, but the design and age of the box made the value skyrocket.

She opened it up—the inside was lined in blue velvet and was just as beautiful as the outside. Belladonna sat up in her lap and sniffed the edge.

"Even Belladonna likes it," Morgan said as the cat pushed her head further into the box.

"Meow." Belladonna poked her paw into the box pushing at the lining, then with a swipe of her claw she ripped the lining from the side of the box.

"Belladonna!" Morgan jerked the box away from the cat. Something that had been hidden inside the lining caught her attention.

She gingerly pulled the small piece of paper out.

"What's that?" Celeste asked.

"Looks like a note." Morgan unfolded the aging paper to reveal old fashioned writing on the inside.

The sea is my love,
The Ocean's Revenge lies below my love.

JOLENE PEERED OVER HER SHOULDER. "What's that mean?"

Morgan put the note on the coffee table. "I'm not sure. The *Ocean's Revenge* was the ship that Isaiah Blackmoore captained."

"Does that mean the ship is below the sea? Like sunken?" Fiona cocked an eyebrow at the note.

"No," Luke said gazing out the window at the Atlantic. "I saw the sonar readings on the treasure hunter's ship and there's no sunken treasure out there."

Morgan frowned at the note. "Maybe it *was* out there once and has since been recovered. I mean the note *was* written three hundred years ago."

"Yeah, you're probably right," Fiona said. "Anyway, I don't know about the rest of you, but I've had enough of pirates and treasure hunts to last me a lifetime—maybe some things are better off staying dead and buried."

"Hear, hear," Celeste said raising her juice glass for a toast.

Morgan clinked her tea mug against the coffee, tea and juice glasses of everyone else. She'd had enough of pirates and treasure too. Besides, with three hundred years of family members and treasure hunters searching for it, the treasure was probably long gone.

Morgan settled back into her chair ignoring the niggling of doubt that was tugging at her gut.

She had everything she needed right in this room … her sisters, her good friends Jake and Cal, Belladonna—and Luke.

And, since it looked like Luke was going to be sticking around for a while, she had a feeling that she wasn't going to be very interested in spending her time digging around for buried treasure … no matter what her gut feeling was telling her.

THE END.

* * *

SIGN UP below for an exclusive never-before-published novella from my Lexy Baker culinary mystery series plus you'll be added to my VIP reader list to get all my latest releases at the lowest discount price:

DID YOU ENJOY THIS STORY? Then you'll want to pick up the rest of the Blackmoore Sisters Cozy Mysteries for your Kindle:

Dead Wrong
Dead & Buried
Dead Tide
Buried Secrets
Deadly Intentions
A Grave Mistake
Spell Found
Fatal Fortune

ALSO BY LEIGHANN DOBBS

Cozy Mysteries

Silver Hollow

Paranormal Cozy Mystery Series

***

A Spell of Trouble (Book 1)

Spell Disaster (Book 2)

Nothing to Croak About (Book 3)

Cry Wolf (Book 4)

Mooseamuck Island Cozy Mystery Series

* * *

A Zen For Murder

A Crabby Killer

A Treacherous Treasure

Mystic Notch

Cat Cozy Mystery Series

* * *

Ghostly Paws

A Spirited Tail

A Mew To A Kill

Paws and Effect

Probable Paws

Blackmoore Sisters

Cozy Mystery Series

* * *

Dead Wrong

Dead & Buried

Dead Tide

Buried Secrets

Deadly Intentions

A Grave Mistake

Spell Found

Fatal Fortune

Lexy Baker Cozy Mystery Series

* * *

Lexy Baker Cozy Mystery Series Boxed Set Vol 1 (Books 1-4)

Or buy the books separately:

Killer Cupcakes

Dying For Danish

Murder, Money and Marzipan

3 Bodies and a Biscotti

Brownies, Bodies & Bad Guys

Bake, Battle & Roll

Wedded Blintz

Scones, Skulls & Scams

Ice Cream Murder

Mummified Meringues

Brutal Brulee (Novella)

No Scone Unturned

Magical Romance with a Touch of Mystery

***

Something Magical

Curiously Enchanted

Romantic Comedy

***

Corporate Chaos Series

In Over Her Head (book 1)

Contemporary Romance

***

Reluctant Romance

Sweet Romance (Written As Annie Dobbs)

Hometown Hearts Series

***

No Getting Over You (Book 1)

***

Sweetrock Sweet and Spicy Cowboy Romance

Some Like It Hot

Too Close For Comfort

———

Regency Romance

* * *

Scandals and Spies Series:

Kissing The Enemy

Deceiving the Duke

Tempting the Rival

Charming the Spy

Pursuing the Traitor

The Unexpected Series:

An Unexpected Proposal

An Unexpected Passion

Dobbs Fancytales:

Dobbs Fancytales Boxed Set Collection

———

Western Historical Romance

***

Goldwater Creek Mail Order Brides:

Faith

American Mail Order Brides Series:

Chevonne: Bride of Oklahoma

———————————

A NOTE FROM THE AUTHOR

I hope you enjoyed reading this book as much as I enjoyed writing it. This is the second book in the Blackmoore sisters mystery series and I have a whole bunch more planned!

The setting for this book series is based on one of my favorite places in the world - Ogunquit Maine. Of course, I changed some of the geography around to suit my story, and changed the name of the town to Noquitt but the basics are there. Anyone familiar with Ogunquit will recognize some of the landmarks I have in the book.

The house the sisters live in sits at the very end of Perkins Cove and I was always fascinated with it as a kid. Of course, back then it was a mysterious, creepy old house that was privately owned and I was dying to go in there. I'm sure it must have had an attic stuffed full of antiques just like in the book!

Today, it's been all modernized and updated—I think you can even rent it out for a summer vacation. In the book the house looks different and it's also set high up on a cliff (you'll see why in a later book) where in real life it's not. I've also made the house much older to suit my story.

Believe it or not, much of the pirate lore I have in the book is actually true! Pirates really did bury treasure all along the east coast and there was a stash of pirate booty dug up in the 1930s in Biddeford like I mention in the book.

Also, if you like cozy mysteries, you might like my book "*Brownies, Bodies & Bad Guys*" which is part of my Lexy Baker cozy mystery series. I have an excerpt from it at the end of this book.

This book has been through many edits with several people and even some software programs, but since nothing is infallible (even the software programs) you might catch a spelling error or mistake and, if you do, I sure would appreciate it if you let me know - you can contact me at lee@leighanndobbs.com.

Oh, and I love to connect with my readers so please   do   visit   me   on   facebook   at http://www.facebook.com/leighanndobbsbooks or at my website http://www.leighanndobbs.com.

Want a free never-before-published novella from my Lexy Baker culinary mystery series? Go to: http://www.leighanndobbs.com/newsletter and enter your email address to signup - I promise never to share it and I only send emails every couple of weeks so I won't fill up your inbox.

ABOUT THE AUTHOR

Leighann Dobbs discovered her passion for writing after a twenty year career as a software engineer. She lives in New Hampshire with her husband Bruce, their trusty Chihuahua mix Mojo and beautiful rescue cat, Kitty. When she's not reading, gardening or selling antiques, she likes to write romance and cozy mystery novels and novelettes which are perfect for the busy person on the go.

Find out about her latest books and how to get her next book for free by signing up at:

http://www.leighanndobbs.com

Connect with Leighann on Facebook and Twitter

http://facebook.com/leighanndobbsbooks

Get in on Leighann's private readers group on Facebook:

https://www.facebook.com/groups/ldobbsreaders/

EXCERPT FROM BROWNIES, BODIES AND BAD GUYS:

Lexy sat at one of the cafe tables next to the picture window in her bakery, *The Cup and Cake*, admiring how the princess cut center stone of her engagement ring sparkled in the midmorning sunlight. She sighed with contentment, holding her hand up and turning the ring this way and that as she marveled at the rainbow of colors that emerged when it caught the light at different angles.

Her thoughts drifted to her fiance, Jack Perillo. Tall, hunky and handsome, her heart still skipped a beat when he walked in the room even though they'd been dating for over a year. Lexy had met Jack, a police detective in their small town, when she'd been accused of poisoning her ex-boyfriend. She'd been proven innocent, of course, and she and Jack had been seeing each other ever since. And now they were getting married.

Movement on the other side of the street caught her attention, pulling her away from her thoughts. Her eyes widened in surprise—it was Jack! *What was he doing here?*

Lexy felt a zing in her stomach. Jack wasn't alone. Lexy's eyes narrowed as she craned her neck to get a better look. He was with a woman. A tall, leggy blonde who was clinging to him like tissue paper clings to panty hose.

Lexy stood up pressing closer to the window, her joy in the ring all but forgotten. Her heart constricted when she saw how the leggy blonde was pawing at Jack, giggling up into his face. *Who the hell was she?* They looked very familiar with each other. Clearly Jack knew her … and it seemed he knew her well.

Jack and the blonde started to walk down the street, out of view. Lexy pushed herself away from the window, stumbling over a chair in her haste to get to the doorway. She spun around, righting the chair, then turned, sprinting toward the door.

She reached out for the handle, jerking back in surprise as the door came racing toward her, almost smacking her in the face.

Standing in the doorway was her grandmother,

Mona Baker, or Nans as Lexy called her. But instead of her usual cheery appearance, Nans looked distraught. Lexy could see lines of anxiety creasing her face and her normally sparkly green eyes were dark with worry.

Lexy's stomach sank. "Nans, what's the matter?"

"Lexy, come quick," Nans said, putting her hand on Lexy's elbow and dragging her out the door. "Ruth's been arrested!"

* * *

"Arrested? For what?" Lexy asked, as Nans propelled her down the street toward her car.

"Nunzio Bartolli was found dead. They think Ruth might have something to do with it!"

Lexy wrinkled her brow. Ruth was one of Nans's best friends. They both lived at the retirement center in town and along with two of their other friends, Ida and Helen, they amused themselves by playing amateur detective solving various crimes and mysteries. The older women were full of spunk and could be a handful, but Lexy had a hard time believing any of them would be involved in a murder. They thrived on *solving* murders, not *committing* them.

"What? How would Ruth even know him?" Lexy

opened the door to her VW beetle and slipped into the driver's seat as Nans buckled up in the passenger seat.

"Nunzio was a resident at the Brook Ridge Retirement Center."

Lexy raised her brows. "He was? I heard he had ties to organized crime."

"Well, I don't know about that. He seemed like a nice man." Nans shrugged, then waved her hand. "Now let's get a move on!"

Lexy pulled out into the street, glancing over at the area where she had seen Jack. She slowed down as she drove by, craning her neck to look down the side street where she thought they had gone, but they were nowhere to be seen.

"Can you speed it up? Ruth needs us." Nans fidgeted in the passenger seat.

"Right. Sorry." Lexy felt a pang of guilt. Of course, helping Ruth was more important than finding out what Jack was up to. It was probably nothing but her overactive imagination anyway. Lexy decided to push the leggy blonde from her mind and focus on Ruth.

"So what happened?"

"I'm not really sure. Ida said the police knocked on Ruth's door early this morning and took her in,"

Nans said, then turned sharply in her seat. "We should call Jack and see if he can help her. Why didn't I think of that before?"

Lexy's stomach clenched at the sound of her fiance's name. She wasn't sure if she wanted to call Jack right now, especially with the image of him and the blonde fresh in her mind. *Should she confront him or let it slide?*

If it was innocent, which it probably was, she'd just make a fool out of herself by confronting him. It was probably a good idea to let some time pass before she talked to him. Lexy was afraid her impulsive nature might cause her to blurt something out she might regret later.

"Hopefully, he'll be at the station. I should call Cassie back at the bakery though, and tell her I've gone out for a while. She'll probably be wondering where I disappeared to." Lexy picked up her cell phone just as she pulled into the parking lot at the police station.

Nans jumped out of the car before she even had it in park. "I'll see you in there."

Lexy watched in amusement as the sprightly older woman sprinted into the station, her giant purse dangling from her arm. She felt sorry for any officer that might try to prevent her grandmother from seeing Ruth.

She made a quick call to Cassie, letting her know where she was and that she'd fill her in later. Then she made her way into the lobby behind Nans.

Nans was talking to Jack's partner, police detective John Darling, who nodded at Lexy as she joined them.

"Ruth isn't arrested!" Nans smiled at Lexy.

Lexy raised an eyebrow at John.

"We just had her in for questioning," John explained.

"Why?"

John rubbed his chin with his hand. "We found her fingerprints and some of her personal effects in Nunzio Bartolli's condo."

Nans gasped. "What? How would those get in there?"

John winked, pushing himself away from the wall he was leaning against. "You'll have to ask Ruth that."

Lexy stared after him as he walked over to the reception desk, his long curly hair hung in a ponytail down his back which swung to the side as he leaned his tall frame over the counter to look at something on the computer. "Actually, she's free to go now. I'll bring her out here if you guys want."

"Please do," Nans said, then turned to Lexy. "Isn't that wonderful? I was so worried."

Lexy nodded as she watched John disappear through the door that led to the offices inside the station. John and her assistant Cassie had been married this past spring and she'd gotten to know him fairly well. She wondered if she should ask him if he knew anything about the blonde she had seen Jack with but didn't want to seem like she was prying into Jack's business.

Lexy shook her head. She needed to stop thinking about the blonde. She trusted Jack. They were getting married, for crying out loud, and she didn't want to be one of those wives who kept her husband on a short leash. The best thing for her to do was to forget all about it.

The door opened and Ruth came out. Nans rushed over giving her a hug. Lexy felt her shoulders relax, relieved that Ruth wasn't in trouble.

"Oh, thanks for coming," Ruth said to Nans and Lexy.

"No problem," Lexy said. "Shall we go? I can drive you guys back to the retirement center, if you want."

"That would be wonderful," Nans said as the three of them made their way to the door. Lexy held it open for the two older women, then followed them out into the summer sunshine.

Ruth breathed in a deep breath of fresh air. "It's good to be outside. For a while there I was a little worried I might be spending my golden years in a cell."

"Why would you think that? Surely you had nothing to do with Nunzio's murder?" Nans raised her eyebrows at Ruth as they walked to Lexy's car.

"Of course I didn't! But they did have some evidence that pointed to me," Ruth said, as she folded herself into Lexy's back seat.

"That's what John said." Lexy slipped into the driver's seat angling the rear view mirror so she could look at Ruth. "What was that all about?"

Lexy saw Ruth's cheeks turn slightly red.

Nans turned in her seat so she could look at Ruth, too. "John said they found your fingerprints and personal effects in Nunzio's condo. How is that possible?"

Ruth turned an even darker shade of red and looked down at her lap, pretending to adjust her seatbelt. "I was in his condo."

"What?" Nans and Lexy said at the same time.

Ruth looked up. Her eyes met Lexy's in the mirror then slid over to look at Nans. "I was seeing Nunzio. Actually, I went there quite regularly. So, naturally, my fingerprints were all over his condo. I was there last night and I must have left a pair of earrings there that the police were somehow able to trace to me."

Nans gasped. "You were there last night? The night he was murdered?"

Ruth nodded. "Yes, I was. But don't worry. I assure you Nunzio was *very* much alive when I left."

Made in the USA
Las Vegas, NV
16 April 2023